Pretty Bones

Pretty Bones

Aya Tsintziras

James Lorimer & Company Ltd., Publishers
Toronto

James Lorimer & Company Ltd., Publishers acknowledges the support of the Ontario Arts Council. We acknowledge the financial support of the Government of Canada through the Canada Book Fund for
our publishing activities. We acknowledge the support of the Canada
Council for the Arts which last year invested $20.1 million in writing
and publishing throughout Canada. We acknowledge the Government
of Ontario through the Ontario Media Development Corporation's
Ontario Book Initiative.

  Canada

Cover Image: iStockphoto

Library and Archives Canada Cataloguing in Publication

Tsintziras, Aya
        Pretty bones / Aya Tsintziras.

(SideStreets)
Issued also in an electronic format.
ISBN 978-1-55277-713-8 (bound).--ISBN 978-1-55277-712-1
(pbk.)

        1.Anorexia nervosa--Juvenile fiction. I.Title. II.Series:
SideStreets

PS8639.S59P74 2011   jC813'.6   C2010-907414-9

James Lorimer & Company Ltd.,   Distributed in the United States by:
Publishers   Orca Book Publishers
317 Adelaide Street West, Suite 1002 P.O. Box 468
Toronto, ON, Canada   Custer, WA USA
M5V 1P9   98240-0468
www.lorimer.ca

Printed and bound in Canada.
Manufactured by Webcom in Toronto, Ontario, Canada in August, 2011.
Job #379094

For my grandpa, Cyril Kalfin,
for knowing this day would come.

Chapter 1

I come home from school to an empty house, something I have become used to. My mother is the editor of the beauty magazine *Facade*, a job that obviously requires a lot of time, but the amount of effort she puts into it is beyond normal. She is the definition of a workaholic — perhaps she even pushes the definition. When I lie awake in bed around midnight, willing sleep to pass over my body, I hear her key in the door, followed by frantic typing on the downstairs computer. If she'd put that much effort into raising me, then hey, maybe I would have turned out alright.

Closing the front door behind me, I look around. We live in a modest two-storey house, despite my eternal longing for an attic room where I can hide. My mom is an avid art fan, so there is artwork all over the walls. This makes it seem as if we're living in a gallery. You would expect me to be absolutely gorgeous from the paintings around me, like the beauty should rub off. You would, in turn, be disappointed.

I put my bag down on the floor and head into the kitchen, searching the contents of the refrigerator for something to shut my stomach up. The grumbling is an orchestra, and it is extremely annoying. Things would be so much easier if your body didn't make noises when you were supposedly hungry. Because, after all, what *is* hunger? You don't need to eat nearly as much to survive as people think. I have been living on coffee and diet sodas and small meals for months now, and I'm still here. I sigh, pushing aside cartons of Chinese food and leftover pizza — all my mom eats is junk food — and settle on a plain yogurt. After a few spoonfuls, I throw it in the garbage and put the spoon in the sink. Life is so much simpler when you reduce the amount of food you eat.

Any stressful situation — and they usually involve food — calls for coffee. Not just any coffee — Nescafé. I boil the water and spoon the powder into a cup, my dad's mug. It used to be bright yellow but has now faded to an almost-white. I keep it in my room, old coffee rings at the bottom and all. I like the stains. They show there's still a piece of him left here.

I go upstairs and pull my scale out from underneath my bed. Stepping onto it, I take a deep breath and close my eyes. Please. Please, let it be a good number.

Heart pounding, I look down.

113.

That's two pounds less than the last time I checked, five days ago. I've been too afraid to check since then. Better, but still not enough.

The doorbell rings and I hastily throw my green Converse sneakers back on. It's Dylan, holding up a McDonald's bag. "Hey," he says. "I brought dinner. I thought we could hang out."

I force a smile. "I just ate, but come on in."

We sit at the kitchen table and Dylan takes out a few cartons, pushing fries toward me. I simply shake my head and he nods, pulling a plastic carton out of the bag. "I got you a salad. You know, it's healthy and all."

What Dylan doesn't realize is that with the dressing, all those calories add up. "Thanks, but I've decided to become a vegetarian. There's chicken in that salad." The whole vegetarianism thing is a cover-up, of course.

He opens his mouth as if to say more, but seems to decide against it. I watch him eat, feeling uncomfortable — scratching my arm, tucking my hair behind my ear. When I yawn, he looks over at me. "What time did you get to sleep last night?"

"Two, three maybe?" I say with a shrug. "I don't know when I actually fell asleep."

I like the way Dylan looks at me. His eyes travel across my face, seeing what he chooses to — whatever good he can find in the mess that I am. He swallows his bite of hamburger and says,

"Maybe you should ask your doctor about that. You can't always have trouble sleeping."

"It's nothing. Just insomnia." I know this isn't true, that days upon days of not getting much sleep can add up, but I don't feel like discussing it further.

"So that's why you frequent Starbucks?" Dylan asks, smiling. "You need the caffeine fix?"

I smile back. "That, and it tastes like heaven."

He laughs, finishes off his hamburger, then eats a few more fries before shoving the carton in the paper bag. I feel like that fat and grease will float through the air and land on my body. I've probably gained ten pounds just from looking at it.

"I think I need a cigarette," I say, fumbling around in my bag until I find my pack of Belmonts.

"I thought you'd given that up." Dylan looks amused.

I shrug. I can't tell him that smoking is an easy way to kill the hunger pangs. I'd much rather he think I'm just as addicted as Matt, the only one in our group who smokes — and I guess, in a way, I am. I stand up, smoothing out my t-shirt. "C'mon, let's go outside. I can't have this in here."

"What if your mom comes home?"

I smirk at the thought. "Yeah, right. She's never here."

He follows me out onto the front porch. It is early evening, darkness tracing the edges of the sky.

Dylan sits down next to me, watching as I slip a cigarette out of the pack, light it, and take a long drag. "If it makes you feel any better," he says, "I haven't seen my mom all week. She's dating this new guy and they're spending all their waking hours together. Same story every time, of course. Soon she'll be back to singing depressing songs in the shower."

I raise my eyebrows. "I'm highly suspicious of people who sing in the shower." When he laughs, I continue, "I'm serious! It's creepy. Stepford-wife kind of creepy."

"Great movie, bad remake."

I nod, taking another drag of my cigarette. "I know! Remakes are like saying you should forget the past. Which is a good lesson and all, but it doesn't exactly work that way."

He glances at me, looking upset. Here it comes, I think. "Raine, I don't really think you should be smoking."

"And don't you think that's just a tiny bit hypo-critical? You smoke sometimes."

"You said that you've become a vegetarian. Isn't that . . . out of health concerns?"

I stare up at the sky — indigo blue with navy bleeding into the centre. Night is coming quickly. "Um. Not really." I have dug myself into a hole. "Meat is just disgusting, alright?" And eliminat-ing meat seems like an easy way to cut down my fat intake.

"Hey, come on," he says, touching my arm and

11

sending shivers through my entire body. "You don't have to get all defensive. It's just me."

I take another drag before I stand up, smoke filling my lungs and doing damage that I don't care to think about. I stamp the cigarette out, throw it into a nearby bush, and turn to Dylan, kissing him softly. There is something wonderful about his kisses. He is my first boyfriend, so I have nothing to compare him to, but I like that he's the only boy I have shared all of this with. Love really is as amazing as everyone makes it out to be.

"I love you," I say. I look at him hard, willing him to realize that I have appointed him my Prince Charming, though I would never admit it.

"I love you too." We kiss again, longer this time, and when we pull away he grins. "There's an empty house behind us and we're out here talking."

Normally I would laugh, say he's being a typical male, but the suggestion is a welcome one. Because as much as I have begun to dislike the fact that sex means being naked, it is a reminder that I am able to feel. And tonight, I need that reminder, that I am something more than just a rumbling stomach. I smile and take his hand.

We fall onto my bed as usual, undressing, but as Dylan lowers himself on top of me, I stare up at my bedroom ceiling, unable to stop the thoughts. Living on the outside and looking in, you are never quite sure what you're looking at, or what you're looking for. You seem to be changing. It happens so fast you can barely make sense of it. All you know is that your collarbones weren't quite so visible, and now they poke out of your skin as if they're trying to break away, leaving your body because it is just too unbearable. All you know, really, is how much you adore your bones. How much you crave them.

After, Dylan kisses my cheek and lies on his back. I lean my head on his chest in the usual place, trying to crawl back to the girlfriend I'm supposed to be. It feels so foreign. I can't stop thinking about how huge I must look.

"You're so beautiful," he whispers.

I never believe this. To the best of my knowledge, I have never been beautiful. Different-looking, maybe, from my female classmates — carbon copies of girls wearing tight jeans and fuzzy boots and showing too much cleavage. My long, straight black hair makes me stand out, along with my so-called bad attitude. But really, life isn't made up of constant sunshine, so why pretend?

When your father dies and you are fifteen years old, you do not like to talk about it. Because of the obvious reasons. Because it hurts. And then there you are at sixteen — almost seventeen, but not quite. You are still at that age that is supposed to be magical and filled with pink. But now you are mentally pulling apart your facial features in the bathroom mirror, changing that pain into something you can see.

I walk to school the next day with Katrina. She has been my best friend since we were young, and we're complete opposites: she has wavy blond hair and a cheery personality. Ever since I met Dylan and Matt — our other friend — at a tenth grade party, it has always been the four of us. We seemed to just collide, splashing into each other like paint on a canvas. I am grateful for their friendship, even if I don't always show it. They make me feel grounded, connected to someone other than my reflection.

As we turn the corner, our school comes into view. It's exactly what you'd picture — a three-storey brick building with a huge front lawn, and a track complete with bleachers for that perfect high school experience of cheerleaders and football games. Okay, well, my school doesn't have a cheerleading team. But we do have what's considered to be the best high school football team in Toronto. Not that I give a crap about sports.

"I know it's only the second day of school, but summer already feels, like, a million miles away," Katrina says as we step onto the bright green grass. "There is a really cute guy in my Spanish class, though."

"Of course," I say with a smirk. "There is always a cute guy."

I follow Katrina into the building and pull my cell phone out of my bag. I'm expecting a text

14

from Dylan. It's a tradition. He sends me a text before school (or before noon if it's summer), telling me he loves me. It's sweet, and I've gotten used to it. Surprisingly, today my inbox is empty.

Strange. He never forgets. At least I have AP English first period. The workload is going to be so intense, which is perfect, because it will give me an excuse whenever I don't feel like going out for dinner with my friends.

A familiar sound rings out, seeming to cloak the air in happiness. My boyfriend's laughter. And I see it at the same time Katrina does: Dylan standing to our left, his arm leaning against the row of lockers behind him, a pretty girl next to him. Tight black pants. Ramones t-shirt. She's new. I would have recognized her skinny body before. That perfect skinny that you don't have to work for. She shakes her short orange hair and looks at Dylan in a way that makes my stomach ache.

"What the hell is this?" Katrina's good mood has turned sour.

My reaction exactly. I take another deep breath, trying to figure out what to do. Should I walk right over and demand to know the meaning of this? Or simply shake it off and find my locker, hoping he'll clue me in later?

Thankfully, I don't have to do either. Dylan spots us standing there three feet away and grins. "Raine! Katrina! Hey guys. Come meet Georgia. She's new."

I force a smile. My instinct is to be totally rude,

but maybe what I saw wasn't the real story. Maybe he was just being nice, trying to make her feel at home. "Welcome," I say, realizing as soon as the word has slipped out of my mouth how lame it sounds.

"Hi," Katrina says, clearing her throat. "What brings you to Lawrence? We don't get many twelfth-grade transfers."

Georgia leans against her locker, and I notice the tattoo of a treble clef on her wrist. Great. She's into music. "I was going to Northern. But then I heard you guys have a great band, so I thought I'd give it a shot. Something to impress the colleges in the U.S., you know?"

My dream is to go to an American Ivy League, or an innovative school like Sarah Lawrence. I try to ignore the dry taste of bitterness in my mouth. "That can be expensive."

"Georgia's dad's pretty huge in the advertising world," Dylan says, giving me a look. His tone is new. It's patronizing, the kind of tone you'd use to talk to a little kid, trying to tell them how the world really is. Well, I'm almost seventeen and I get the memo.

Chapter 2

"How was your morning?" Katrina asks me at lunch, taking a bite of her chocolate chip cookie. We sit in our usual formation — she and Matt on one side, Dylan and I across from them.

"Amazing. AP English is going to be so great this year," I say, taking a sip of my Diet Coke. "What about you?"

"Boring, as usual. I hate school. But I'm so excited to try out for the musical! It's *Grease* this year."

Dylan smiles. "Well, we can't all be as smart as Raine."

Katrina feigns shock. "Are you calling me a dumb blond?"

"He's just complimenting his girlfriend. Which is understandable, considering how the two of them are such a sickeningly cute couple." Matt grins between mouthfuls of a hot dog. I can't believe how my friends can just eat junk food without a second thought.

"We're not cute," I say, making a face.

Katrina pushes half of her chicken sandwich toward me. "You look hungry," she says.

And my stomach rumbles as if on cue. We look at each other and I think, *shit*. I swallow a gulp of Diet Coke. "No, not really." I stand up, absolutely starving, and try not to look at Matt's hot dog. "I really need a cup of coffee. I'm going to Starbucks."

"Oh, I'll go with you," Katrina says, standing up too.

The air is warm on our skin when we get outside. I like the poetry of the seasons, the way they change. I'm glad September is closing in on us. The happiness of wearing tank tops and miniskirts is lost on me. I'd rather stay hidden, like Rapunzel in her tower with her blankets of golden curls. If she was ever worried about her body, she could just cover it up with all that hair.

Katrina chatters on about the cute boy in her Spanish class. I feel completely isolated. We are both such different people now. Or maybe only I am, and that makes it seem like she has changed too. My life now, with its headaches and sad songs, feels very confusing.

***

Some people's living rooms are stuffy and barely lived-in, but mine is comfortable, adorned with modern furniture and antique touches. For all her perpetual absence, my mom sure has taste. The first Saturday afternoon in October, I lie down on the couch, listening to my CD player. I was over iPods the second they came out. I like my music loud, convincing myself that the lyrics and melodies can cancel out my life and calm me down forever.

I close my eyes for a few minutes, suddenly so tired. Then my mom is pulling an earphone off my head. "What?" I ask drowsily.

"I've been calling you for ages. Didn't you hear me?" She pauses, looking at my CD player. "I guess you didn't. Doesn't that loud music give you a headache?" I swear, there must be a book where all mothers get their lines. Don't they get tired of preaching about the same things, like "make sure you eat enough protein and do all your homework and get enough sleep"? They should really say stuff like "watch out or you'll fall through the cracks in the mirror and your own insanity."

"No, it doesn't give me a headache. I love Alanis," I say. I try to be patient around my mother, but sometimes I just feel like yelling at her. She never says what she really feels.

"What about Nirvana? I thought they were your favourite band."

"Okay. Number one, that's Dylan's favourite band. And number two, what's with all the mother-daughter small talk? Do you need something?"

"Can't we just have a normal conversation?" she asks.

"The last time we had a conversation it was you yelling at me because I came home too late from a date with Dylan."

She ignores this, leaning against the doorframe. "I was about to order some takeout. What do you feel like? Pizza? Chinese? Or there's that Thai place that just opened up."

I instinctively put my hand over my stomach, poised to stop the rumbles that thankfully don't occur. "You're never home for dinner."

"I thought maybe we could spend some time together."

I don't answer. When has she ever wanted this?

"We haven't done that for a while," she continues.

"Yeah, a while."

My mom sighs. "Why are you in a bad mood? Did something happen at school today?"

"Get with the program, *Marion*," I say. "I'm in a perpetual bad mood. Look, I have some homework to do, and small talk really isn't on my agenda." I gesture at the pile of books sitting on the coffee table.

"What if it's on mine?" she asks, looking wounded.

If she's going to guilt-trip me, I'm so leaving the room.

She sighs again, louder this time, and sits down on the big leather chair. I have a sudden flash of being five years old and sitting with my dad in that chair. It was always his seat, where he watched baseball. That's what my memories of him are: random and fleeting. Some things are crystal clear, as if they happened yesterday, but others are clouded up with nothing but time. Time is supposed to heal things, but that's just another cliché.

"Why do you *act* like this?" she asks. "I'm making an effort here. I'm sorry I haven't been around lately —"

"If lately means the past two years . . ." I say, cutting her off.

"The office has been crazy this week." She is making excuses, instead of admitting that this house makes her feel too sad. "I'd appreciate a little understanding here. It's not . . . easy doing all of this on my own."

I look at this woman who seems so foreign to me. Her hair, black like mine, is cut in a piecey, choppy bob. Her bangs are pushed to the side whereas I wear mine straight down. Her style is too trendy for someone who talks like she lives in the Middle Ages. Her red lipstick, her gold bangles, her black high heels — none of these things are familiar. We pass each other in the mornings, her drinking coffee before work and me avoiding breakfast. I dash out the door before she can say anything.

"This is a stupid conversation," I say.

I go up to the bathroom and stare in the mirror the way I always do, but this time it's for a different reason. I am trying to remember. What was I like before all of this started, the year I was fifteen? I know I weighed more, of course, and I was obsessed with red lipstick, and I only wore my hair in a ponytail.

This began as just a diet, something neat and tidy, something that seemed so simple. And then a switch clicked on and it became a part of me. Once I started eating less, I expected to think about food less too, but no such luck. Food is always on my mind. There are so many rules, so many things I can't eat because they have too many calories. Maybe nothing is safe, maybe only water, and maybe not even that.

So, yes. I know what I'm doing to myself. But I'm fine. I could stop if I wanted to.

I just don't want to. Not yet.

***

That night, I hear the doorbell. I open the door to find Dylan standing on my front porch. "Hey," he says.

"Hi." Everything slows down. Dylan just smiles at me and says, in a voice so soft it's almost a whisper, "*I am all yours, so please be all mine.*"

"I like that you still remember those lyrics."

"Hey, it's a good song."

In grade eleven, when The Used came out with a song called "Earthquake," I played it for Dylan because I knew he would love it. He decided it would be "our song."

Once we're upstairs, Dylan lies down on my bed and I follow, resting my head in the crook of his shoulder. He kisses the top of my head. My black t-shirt is riding up slightly, and Dylan slowly starts to tickle my stomach. Soon he's lying on top of me while I shriek with laughter. "Stop!" I say, out of breath, and when he does he smiles and kisses me. This is so much like the way it used to be. I think about how just seconds ago he was touching my fat. I manage to push the thought out of my mind, focusing instead on Dylan. His hand inches its way underneath my shirt. I see this moment as a great splash of bright yellow, a chance at happiness, something to bottle up and keep forever.

We sit up, Dylan slipping my t-shirt over my head. He takes his own shirt off and I reach over to undo his jeans. Our clothes now in heaps on the floor, we keep kissing, and I lie back on the bed, pulling him on top of me.

***

While Dylan sleeps, I think about how beautiful he looks. I can see the dreams playing across his face, the places he must be travelling to without moving one inch.

I drift off eventually. Around four, I open my eyes to find Dylan's staring right back at me. My mom is a heavy sleeper, so I don't expect she's noticed that he's here. "Hi," I say. I notice my comforter has slipped down, showing my stomach, and pull it back up to my chin. No matter how hard I try, my stomach always looks huge.

"Hey," he says, pulling me closer and kissing my cheek. "That was pretty amazing." He smells the way violets would smell under an overcast sky. He turns onto his side and rests on one elbow, tracing my shoulder with his free hand. "I'm so lucky to be with you," he whispers.

"How come?" I ask.

"If you saw yourself as half as incredible as the way I see you . . ."

"I'm not incredible."

"Come on, don't say that kind of stuff." He reaches over to touch my side. "There is no one else for me, okay? Just you." He leans down and kisses my forehead, emphasizing his point.

Maybe, if we can continue on like this, if he can always tell me how perfect I am for him, I might start to believe it. "Okay," I say, thinking that since I've said it, I may as well act like it's true. My whole existence is wrapped up in pretending, after all. Pretending I don't miss my dad. Pretending I don't miss my mom.

"Have you been writing any new songs lately?" I ask.

"Yeah. I wrote one on the subway the other night. You always show me all these new things — movies, music. So I started coming up with lyrics about you, and how it's like you let me enter this . . . new world."

"Wow. You wrote a song about me?"

"What's the fun of having a boyfriend with a band if he never writes something about you?" He does have a point. "Hey, before I forget . . . we're playing tomorrow night."

"I'll definitely be there."

"Cool. We're all gonna grab a bite to eat afterwards."

I think fast, trying to find a way to get out of it. Ordering salad or saying I'm not hungry can only work for so long. "Um, what's tomorrow's date?" I ask.

"The fourteenth."

"I might . . . have something else going on."

"Like what?"

"Like homework or something. A project, a test." While in the midst of making up excuses, my words seem to get all mixed up.

His voice is teasing, but there is a trace of hurt in it. "My own girlfriend doesn't want to see me play?"

"It's not that . . . it's just . . ."

"What is it?" He's a gentle person, sounding even softer right now. I don't answer, mostly because I feel like I have rocks in my throat. Dylan begins counting off reasons on his fingers. "You're not shy, you dig my music, I wrote this song about you. This totally romantic song, might I add. All your friends are going. Afterwards, we're going to —" He pauses. I hold my breath as he struggles to put the pieces together. "Is it because we're going out for dinner afterwards?" His hand drops.

I'm staring at the floor so I can't see his face as he whispers, "Raine . . ."

"Don't say anything, okay?"

"How can I *not* say anything? Don't you ever look in the *mirror*?"

"That's the fucking problem!" I am on the verge of tears.

"No, the problem is you don't look close enough."

"Oh, and what's really there, Mr. Know-It-All?"

"A too-thin girl who's bony in all the wrong places." Dylan shakes his head, getting worked up. "You don't need to diet."

I roll my eyes. "How do you know what I need?" He touches my arm, but I flinch as soon as the contact is made. "Don't," I say coldly.

Dylan's voice reminds me of homemade vanilla ice cream, calm and quiet and sweet. "I'm sorry for yelling, alright? I worry about you. Katrina does too. She mentioned something the other day."

"What do you want me to say?"

"That you'll come see me play tomorrow night and eat something."

Well, "something" could be anything. It could be a garden salad, a carrot, half of a muffin . . . "Where is everyone going afterwards?"

Dylan sighs. "I don't know. I don't see what the big deal is. It's just a bunch of us getting together and hanging out."

"It's an extremely big deal! If I'm annoying you so much, then why don't you just break up with me?"

He stares at me with a pained look. There is so much silence in the room I think it'll swallow us both whole. The tiny clock on my bedside table measures our lives, taking moments away. There is nothing I want more than for us to stay together, so I don't know why I just said that. But how much I eat or don't eat is none of his business. "What? Are you trying to figure out why you love me?" I pause, and say slowly, "So am I."

Dylan looks trapped, a little boy lost in the streets, unable to find his family. I'm trying to avoid his miserable gaze, but I can feel his cappuccino eyes begging me to stop this. I don't say anything. I can't. I hear him stand up, his dirty black Cons squeaking as he gathers up his stuff, the movements of a boy I have cared about so much. He is polite. He doesn't slam the door behind him. I am very aware of my loneliness now.

I lie down and pull my comforter over me, immediately feeling guilty. Dylan has enough to worry about. His parents are both dating new people after being divorced for years. His advertising exec dad refuses to support Dylan's music. I should be a better, more supportive girlfriend.

It feels like the world has ended. Now it's just coffee and reflections and scales. And I'm left with just the bare bones.

Chapter 3

"Happy birthday!" I feel hands over my eyes and Dylan's familiar voice fills the hallway. It's Monday morning and the day that also happens to be my seventeenth birthday.

"It *is* October fifteenth, is it not?" he asks, his eyebrows furrowed, making him seem so much older. "And I *do* have the best present ever hiding behind my back, do I not? Such a great present that my girlfriend will forget I acted like a jerk?" He grins like a little boy and pulls out a brightly wrapped red package.

I tear off the paper to find a brand new copy of Rebecca Godfrey's *The Torn Skirt*, my favourite book, and a photograph. I look closely to see myself sitting cross-legged on Dylan's bed, writing furiously in a notebook and concentrating very hard.

He points to the book first and says, "It's a new edition. There's some stuff in the back — an interview, I think, and a list of what she likes to read." He points toward the picture. "I thought that might remind you of how much you love writing. You can get started again."

"How do you know that I've stopped?" I ask.

"I can see it in your eyes. You get so calm when you write, and lately . . ." He catches my gaze and I'm the one to look away.

"You just couldn't let this be only about my birthday?" I shake my head, starting toward my locker.

He places his hand on mine, warmth spreading over me. "Look, don't get mad at me, okay? But I don't think you need to be on a diet. If you're worried about school, that's crazy. You're brilliant and you'll get into any school you apply to."

He thinks I'm worried about applying to university? We could be living on separate planets.

I spot Katrina coming over and wave, glad for the distraction. I don't know what the right thing to say to Dylan is.

"Okay, so it's your birthday — happy birthday, by the way! — and I totally think we need to have a party, don't you?" Katrina's habit of jumping into conversations without saying hello first is part of her charm. "Your mom's going to be away all weekend for that magazine thing, right?"

"Right," I say. "We could have a party at my house."

"Oh, Dylan, your band was totally amazing last night!" Katrina gushes. "You should play at the party!"

"That would be cool," he says.

"It's too bad you missed it," Katrina says to me. "Dylan said you have a test today."

I nod. I spent last night holed up at Starbucks, doing homework. Much easier than listening to a million questions about why I wasn't eating. It was worth it, even if I have to deal with this awkward moment.

"Hey, I haven't seen too much of you lately, since you're always busy with the musical," I tell Katrina. "How are you?"

"Oh my gosh! It's totally insane. But I met this awesome guy! Adam. He's playing Danny. He asked me out!"

"That's great!" I smile the biggest smile I can manage, and wonder why this isn't easier. I should be happy for my best friend, but I can't feel it. Katrina is lucky; she owns sunshine and bright colours, things lost to me these days.

The bell rings. "See you later," I say, and walk down the hall.

***

Saturday night comes quickly, bringing with it cool-smelling air, dreams tangled up in the breeze. Katrina arrives first, an hour early, when I've just gotten out of the shower. I answer the door in my robe. She is holding a tiny black dress in one hand and a striped gold and white one in the other. "I don't know what to wear."

"Whatever. You'll look gorgeous," I say. "Besides, you've got Adam. You don't need to impress him."

She rolls her eyes, but I can't relate to her dilemma. My closet is full of plaid shirts and dark dresses. You wouldn't catch me in anything tighter than my favourite pair of faded black jeans. "Boys always need to be impressed," she says. "I think I'll swing by the store to stock up on junk food. Sound good?" When I nod she gives me a quick smile before adjusting her gold sequined purse on her shoulder and going back outside.

I go up to my bedroom and open my closet. I decide on black jeans and a long grey sweater.

The doorbell rings and I take my cup of coffee with me downstairs to answer it. It's Matt, holding two six-packs of beer and grinning. "Hey," he says. "Happy birthday. Where's Katrina?"

"Oh, she went to buy some snacks." *I haven't eaten a single thing all day*, I think, and then rub my forehead. *Don't think about it.* I drink more coffee.

"Good." Matt follows me into the kitchen and watches me as I sit down. "You look great, by the way. Let me guess . . . the grunge era?"

I smile. "Thanks, but these are just my clothes. You don't look so bad yourself, although you're still not matching your shirt to your pants. Katrina will probably kill you."

Matt dresses in his own unique way, though the combinations are often odd. He mixes in skater

31

and trendy and gangster and still manages to look hot.

"I kind of just threw this on. I figure it might be coming off later." He grins at me and raises an eyebrow.

"Ha," I say. "Looks like someone has plans. You *are* the star quarterback, though, so you are definitely in character."

"Well, it's a party, Miss Raine. Sex and drugs and rock 'n' roll."

I laugh and sip my coffee. I notice Matt staring at me and suddenly feel self-conscious. "What?" I ask.

"Uh . . . nothing." He shakes his head, still looking at my body. "It's just, you look thin. Really thin."

"Sure." I take a really big sip of my coffee just to have something to do. An unspoken anxiety fills the room, the two of us enveloped in the absence of sound. I can't think of anything to say to lighten up the moment.

"You know, Dylan's pretty worried. He thinks you have an eating disorder."

"What?" I ask, now so natural in my denial that I almost convince myself. "That's just him being overprotective. You know how boyfriends get."

"It's not just Dylan. It's Katrina, too. And me."

What are they doing, holding group discussions about me? "I really don't know what you're talking about." I stand up. "I have to use the bathroom."

"Hey, come on. We're your friends, alright?" Matt touches my arm, then stands up and puts his hand on my back. "We're just concerned here. We want to make sure that you're eating." He pauses. "How much do you weigh?"

"Matt, shut up, okay? None of your business."

The door opens then, Katrina using the spare key she's had for years.

"Here, let me help you with that." Matt glares at me before walking over to get the food from Katrina. I know all three of us hear my stomach rumble loudly.

Dylan arrives at eight o'clock when my house is already filled with people. He could be dressed as Kurt Cobain, his idol, or just wearing his usual clothes. He says the grunge era was full of a complicated simplicity that our generation is sorely lacking, something I agree with. He kisses me long and slow. "Happy birthday again," he says into my neck, wrapping his arms around me. I breathe in his scent of acoustic guitar notes and pine trees. "You feel skinny, Raine."

I take a deep breath. "Please don't say that."

He nods, and I know I'm home free, at least for tonight. People seem to be arriving every minute, bringing food and more alcohol. I grab a beer and slip away into the pantry off the kitchen, quickly pulling the door closed. I used to love birthdays, the chance to start fresh, begin another year. My dad used to throw me themed parties. The last one was for my eighth birthday, revolving around magic. The rest just blurs, like fog on the windows. Now I just want to wake up one morning and be someone else.

I hear a voice, the only one that matters. I open the pantry door a little to see Dylan standing near the counter with a familiar-looking girl. She's tall, with wavy orange hair, wearing a short black dress. "I haven't felt like practising," he tells her, and that's when the pieces fall into place and I realize she's the new girl in school, and also in his band. I forget her name, something to do with a country or state.

She reaches for his hand and he lets her. *What?*

"You've been ignoring me."

"Georgia," he says, so soft I have to strain to hear.

"I've been confused too. Did you expect we would hook up? I've wanted you for a while now but . . . to have it actually happen . . ." She leans forward and kisses him, and I spill beer all over my clothes. *Hook up?*

Dylan pulls away, shaking his head, and I see that he's crying. "I love her, okay? I can't be with you. I'm with Raine."

"But we have this insane connection, Dyl, don't you feel it?" Georgia looks hurt.

"It doesn't matter what I feel! Shit, George, that shouldn't have happened. We shouldn't have hung out after the gig. It was wrong."

"Well, I'm around. I'm just going to keep trying until I get you," she says, and smiles before leaving the kitchen.

Dylan stands there limply and then heads toward the living room. I can't see either of them anymore, which means they can't see me. I slip out of the pantry and run through the crowd and up to my room, slamming the door shut.

I fall onto the floor, lying down and hugging my knees. This can't be real. Dylan and Georgia. Georgia and Dylan. My heart feels like it's going to fall out of my chest.

A knock sounds on the door. "Raine?" Katrina asks. "Are you in there?" I don't answer, don't move. I hear a male voice say, "She's probably taking a break. Come on, let's get more beer." Probably Adam. I hear their footsteps as they go back downstairs.

I can't face anyone. Not tonight. So I crawl into bed, turn on some music, and close my eyes, trying not to picture the one image I suddenly can't get out of my head: my perfect boyfriend, the person I love more than anyone else, kissing another girl.

Chapter 4

Sunday comes. I spend the afternoon at the library writing a paper for my World Issues class. By four o'clock, I'm way too hungry to concentrate, and walk home, shivering in the fall air. My phone rings — the fourth time Dylan has called me today, and the fourth time I've ignored his call. I turn my phone off.

There is an unfamiliar car in the driveway. I'm curious — did my mother sell her black Lexus and buy a BMW? I unlock the front door and see two half-empty glasses of red wine on the coffee table, a pair of men's brown loafers on the mat. I swallow a few times, try to stay calm, and start up the stairs.

Sure enough, I hear giggles and a deep male voice coming from the direction of my mother's bedroom. Her door is left open and I turn away fast, but not fast enough. My mother is having sex with a man I've never seen before.

"Wait, I hear something," he says.

My mother notices me standing by the stair-case. She claps a hand over her mouth. I close my eyes and grit my teeth while listening to the sounds of them scrambling to get dressed.

"Raine —" she begins, walking into the hall-way and tying up her purple robe.

"Shit!" I yell, too surprised to say more.

The man comes out too. He says, "I think I'll make some coffee," and heads downstairs.

"How long has this been going on?" I ask. "Who *is* he?"

"His name is Ben," she says, and I can tell she's trying her best to compose herself, but her cheeks are flushed, her perfect hair now a mess. "We've been together for . . . a while."

"Thanks. I really appreciate the heads-up. Next time you're going to entertain men in your bed-room, maybe you should consider closing the door first."

"We're getting married," my mom says, her voice breaking. She fidgets with her hands like she's not quite sure where to put them.

I shake my head. This is ridiculous. "Do me a favour and never talk to me again, would you?"

As I walk to my room, my mother follows me, putting her hand on my arm. "Please listen to me," she says, face pleading. "I was going to tell you soon, I was just worried about how you would re-act. We didn't just meet — he is very special to me."

"It's only been two years," I say, unable to stop the tears. "When did you meet him? It must have been . . ."

My mother looks as awful as I feel when the realization dawns on me.

"Did you cheat on dad?" I ask, feeling a new wave of anger.

"I wouldn't . . . put it that way," she says. "Yes, we did meet shortly before the . . . accident. But life isn't so black and white, Raine."

"His name was *Jason*!" I shout. "And it was a *car* accident! It wasn't his fault, it was just terrible luck, and you can never even talk about it! And now, what? You're marrying some guy that you never bothered to introduce me to, and I'm supposed to be thrilled for you?"

I slam my bedroom door before she has a chance to respond. Twenty minutes later, I hear the front door closing, and a car pulling away. Great. At least my mother knows enough to leave me alone right now.

My stomach grumbles, reminding me that I was planning on having a tiny snack, so I head down to the kitchen and search the cupboards. But I'm too upset to think clearly. Before I know it, I'm tearing through a package of chocolate chip cookies, a tub of ice cream, the leftover Chinese cartons in the fridge. And then I throw up, my body doing it for me. I curl up on my side, closing my eyes. I'm lying in vomit, but I'm too exhausted to move.

I hear the door being unlocked — my mother

is home. "Oh my God!" she shouts, rushing over. "What happened?"

I sit up slowly. "I was . . . eating dinner. Maybe I'm coming down with something?"

"I will clean this up," she says, and I watch as she does. Minutes of silence pass. "You know, Raine, the way you're eating is scaring me. To-morrow morning I'm calling your doctor to ask if he can recommend a good family therapist."

"What?" I ask, standing up. "That's not neces-sary! You can't just waltz in here and decide to actually be interested in my life."

"If you don't want to go to family therapy, then you're going alone. End of discussion." When I don't answer, my mother sits down on a kitchen stool and rubs her forehead. "You have a lot of anger and it will be good for you to talk to some-one. I can pick you up from school tomorrow at three o'clock and drive you over."

"Fine. Whatever. I'll go, okay?" I roll my eyes and head toward the staircase, wanting a shower. Wanting to erase this entire day. Wanting to never have known that soon my mother will remarry, and there will be another grown-up in this house to ignore me.

Chapter 5

You could say this therapy business is a non-event. My mother parks a block away and insists on walking me into the office. But when we reach the lobby, her phone rings. "I have to take this," she says, and walks a few feet away for some privacy. A minute later she comes back. "I have to go back to work, something came up. You can take the subway afterwards, right?" I nod. She smiles and says, "Call if you need me."

I watch her walk outside and down the block toward her car. I wait a good five minutes, then push open the sliding glass doors and take the subway. But I don't go home. I go to Starbucks.

I'm hit with another burst of anger as I push open the door. How could she do this? How could she be interested in another guy, while still with my dad? They were in love. I know they were. Every night when I went to bed I heard them in the living room, staying up late drinking wine and talking.

I order a venti non-fat latte and sit at my favourite table, the one in the back away from the window, and pull out my copy of *White Oleander*. The book is beautifully written, almost like poetry. I have never read such a stunning story. The words drip with beauty, and I just want to crawl inside the pages.

The coffee hurts my stomach, pain shooting up from everywhere at once. I wince, closing my eyes briefly, then drink more of my latte, hoping it will stop.

"Janet Fitch. Cool." I look up to find a guy standing at my table — a cute one. He is tall and skinny, clad in a long black trench coat and dark jeans. His black hair falls in clumps, pieces sticking straight up, and he has very pale skin. These things make him seem both neat and messy. He nods at the book in my hands before speaking again. "Sorry, I know this seems kind of creepy, some random guy coming up to you, but that's one of my favourite books." He pauses, smiling. "Is this your first time reading it?"

"Try millionth," I say with a weak smile; it feels funny on my lips, not quite belonging there. "I like to read it every few months because it's so layered. There are so many parts of Astrid's story that I'm always afraid I've missed something."

"The film's a pretty good representation," he says, confidently pulling up a chair and sitting across from me, as if my response was an invitation for him to join me. "As far as books being turned into movies go, I guess. Sometimes I think you should just keep the two things separate." When I nod, he asks, "How old are you?"

"Seventeen. Why?"

"Just curious. You seem kind of older . . . Maybe it's your hair."

"My hair?"

"It's really black. That tends to make people look more mature. So is this your last year of high school?"

"Yup. Grade twelve."

"Awesome," he says, his eyes on mine. "All that high school bullshit is finally almost over. I swear, it drove me crazy." The intent way he's looking at me makes me feel like we're making a real connection, over such dumb conversation as senior year.

"I kind of hate it too, I guess. I mean, the politics of it . . . all the stupid people who think they're better than you, or prettier than you, or . . . whatever."

He smiles. "I doubt those stupid people are prettier than you. When people are idiots, I think it cancels out their looks." When I don't answer, he continues, "Some people are pretty stupid, even after they graduate. I'd love to say it changes, but it doesn't. So what's your name?" It's strange to have a boy that isn't Dylan looking at me. In that way, I mean, like someone else is trying to figure you out, trying to get to know you.

"Raine." I don't hesitate in answering. For whatever reason, I've been waiting for him to ask this all along.

"Cool. I'm Andrew." He puts out his hand and I shake it, smiling a little at the formal gesture, and how informal the rest of him is. He glances nervously around Starbucks. "You know what time it is?"

I reach into my bag and check my cell phone. "Um, four-thirty."

"Shit," Andrew says, standing up quickly. "I'm already late." He smiles at me. "It was nice . . . talking to you."

I watch as he leaves through the back door, heading toward the subway. I stare at the door for a while, wondering where he's going, what it is that he's supposed to be doing.

I get back to my book but something feels different. It's like I'm different, and I don't know why.

***

I skip the cafeteria the next day and spend my lunch hour in the library. I spread out my textbook and a package of sour candy. I'm about halfway through the Calculus problems when I hear Dylan say, "Hey."

"Hey," I say, reluctantly putting down my pencil. "What are you doing here?"

"I just wanted to see you." Dylan leans close and kisses me. He tastes like sunflowers. He doesn't know what's wrong. He doesn't even know something is wrong. He sits down beside me and his gaze falls on my bag of candy. "Is that your lunch?"

I pick up my pencil again and start on another question. "I'll get something later. I'm doing Calculus now."

Dylan fiddles with a hole in his ripped jeans. "I don't see you eat anymore."

I sigh, looking up at him, his brown eyes resembling cups of coffee and muddy soil. I dump a few candies into my hand and stuff them into my mouth. I smirk at him before starting on my homework again.

"Don't be a smartass. This is serious."

"My whole life is serious." I stare at him — his light blue jeans, his white t-shirt, the freckle on his right arm — willing him to stop. "It's pretty serious that you made out with *Georgia*, too."

I've been running through this conversation in my mind, trying to choose words, but I've come up with nothing. It's all too broken, pieces of what could have been haunting my dreams.

Dylan lets out a deep breath, like the air leaving a blow-up pool toy. "Oh man," he whispers. "Where . . ."

"I heard you at the party. Shit, you really know how to make a girl feel welcome in her own home." When he doesn't answer I shake my head.

"Are you going to apologize, at least?"

"Look . . ." As soon as he speaks tears spill down my cheeks. "Of *course* I'm sorry. It was the biggest mistake of my life! I don't even know why I did it."

"You like her. That's why."

I'm testing him because I'm curious, and sure enough, Dylan is quick to deny. "Not even a little bit. I love you."

"She likes you, at least." I take a deep breath. "It's too much."

"We need to talk about this," he says. "You shouldn't have to deal with this, not with all your problems . . ."

"My problems?" I ask, wanting to hit him. "Thanks a lot. You don't even know what's going on with me."

He moves closer, putting his hand on my arm, pulling it away just as quickly. "So tell me."

He looks so earnest that I decide to. "I always have a stomach ache. My mother is never home, and now all of a sudden I found out she has this *fiancé*. And, hey, she cheated on my dad with him!"

I'm not supposed to say that stuff, not out loud. Who says? She does. My other self, the other me, whoever that is. She says. She has me locked in her hold and I can't break free. She is part best friend, part saviour, part torturer. And she is the worst parts of me, brought out into the open.

"Whoa," Dylan says, breathing in deeply. "That's kind of . . . unexpected."

"Yeah, well, I didn't expect to walk in on them, you know . . ." I shiver with the memory. "That's how I found out. Nice, huh. Sound familiar?"

He winces. "I know you. You're strong. I see it in you all the time. This sucks, for sure, but you're going to be okay."

Whenever someone says that, I want to ask how they can be so confident in their ability to see into the future. Life can change quickly, one minute you have something and the next, you just don't.

It is quiet between us. "What do we do now?" Dylan finally asks.

"I don't know," I say. What I want to ask is, if I don't know who my boyfriend is, how am I ever supposed to figure out my own self?

"Maybe this isn't the best time to bring this up, but I'm just going to say it. I'm worried about you." His voice is tired, like it's being pulled by some greater power. He puts his hand on my arm.

I pause for a moment, feeling myself settle into his touch. Sometimes my need for him is so great I'm afraid it's going to swallow me whole. I pull away harshly. "Please just . . . don't. Can you tell me why you kissed her?"

He is silent. We stare at each other and it feels stiff, the air full of Styrofoam. When he begins to speak, his voice sounds like broken glass is caught between the words. "Sometimes I think . . . you take me for granted. You take *us* for granted."

"When have I ever taken you for granted?" I ask, stunned. "How can you *say* that? You . . . me

. . . it's, like, the one important thing."

The bell rings, loud as always. Dylan runs a hand through his messy hair, light brown and shaggy, a gesture that I always find adorable. "I'm sorry," he says. "That was unfair. It's just . . . I don't really know what to do. I want to help."

He didn't do this to hurt me. I know that. But I also know he doesn't know how to help me, and I don't know what to say to fix this.

"We need to take some time apart," I say. "I need to think. But don't worry about me. Okay?" I reach across the table and put my hand over his. There is something so beautiful and powerful about his hands. When he touches me, it's like he is sharing some of that power with me, yet still keeping enough for himself. My own are starting to look bony, and if the light hits them just right you can see the blue veins like rivers across my pale skin.

"Are you sure everything is alright?" When I nod, so does he. "Alright. I trust you."

Dylan saying he trusts me is like parents telling their teenagers not to throw a party when they go away. And I, clad in my anorexia as if it were a pair of black cowboy boots, will starve nonetheless.

***

Mid-November, I wake up early on a Tuesday morning and go into the kitchen to make coffee.

Ben is sitting in his green plaid robe, reading the newspaper. *Thanks for the heads-up, Marion,* I think. I ignore him and spoon Nescafé into my favourite mug. He peers at me over the Business section and asks, "Instant coffee? How can you stand it?"

Okay, this is not cool. Some stranger is sitting in *my* house, making fun of something that connects me to my dad? I give him a cheesy grin. "Gee, I don't know. How can you stand breaking up people's families?"

"Things are not always what they seem," he says. "Every family and couple is different. People are so fascinating, don't you think?"

I meant he is butting in on *this* family, not on the families he works with at his law firm. I finish making my coffee and slink back upstairs to my room. All I can focus on is school, so I pull out my Calculus notebook and go over today's homework. I have to stop every so often and take a series of deep breaths, trying to halt the panic that has taken up residence in my body along with twinges of loneliness. Since November began, Ben is here all the time. He doesn't seem to have officially moved in, but since my mother doesn't speak to me these days, I wouldn't know.

When I get home from school I perform my usual weighing ritual, which means taking my scale out from under my bed and stepping onto the tiny white square. I do this maybe a million times a day. My scale is like a second skin.

A knock sounds on my bedroom door and I quickly slide the scale back into its hiding place. "Come in!" I yell. In waltzes my mother, looking amazing in a deep purple dress and the black sweater I borrow sometimes without her knowing. She is so skinny, does she have to rub it in? "What do you want?"

"I have something important to discuss with you," she says, sitting down on my bed. "Ben is moving in this weekend. We have planned the wedding for the end of June. I'd like you to be a bridesmaid."

I laugh. It's just too good not to. "What?"

"You're my daughter. You should be in the wedding party."

Standing at the altar with my mother and her soon-to-be new husband does not sound like a party. "Fine," I say, "but only if I can invite my friends."

"Of course!" She comes to life now, smiling big. "You may invite whomever you like."

I breathe in deeply, thinking I must have gained at least five pounds just from this conversation. "Okay."

"Good." She stands up and walks over and puts both hands over mine. I flinch. "Ben wants to have a relationship with you. You could try to be nicer to him."

But do you want a relationship with me? I want to ask. "You are such a bitch," I say.

She looks completely taken aback. "Raine!"

"You randomly tried to force me into therapy, but you have no idea that I didn't even go!" I shout.

"Why would you do that?" she asks, shaking her head. "I'm trying, but I can't do this myself. I don't know how to help . . ."

"You can help by leaving my room," I say. I close my eyes so I don't have to look at her, and soon hear heels click-clacking their way down the hallway.

I suppose most mothers would still make their teenage daughters lunch to bring to school, or at least fix an afternoon snack. My mother can call me angry all she wants, but she's right. She can't help, not if she can't even say what's wrong with me out loud.

To understand the whole story, to really and truly get it, you have to consider the kind of person my mother is. She grew up in a small town, got good grades, never stayed out past her curfew of nine o'clock — or so she says. You get the picture. She met my dad at university and they started a whirl-wind romance that displeased both sets of parents. Marion the goody two-shoes English major marry-ing Jason the free spirit actor? Her parents would have nothing to do with them, which explains why I met my grandparents only once, at the funeral. A funeral is a strange place for a fifteen-year-old. There was too much black, and I was suddenly sur-rounded by strangers. And my mother? She never even shed one tear. At least, not in front of me.

If only I could actually see a difference in my body, then all of this starving might have a purpose. But my stomach sticks out and my legs aren't the elegant kind that look good in high heels.

My scale tells me I weigh 103 pounds. I step off and step on again, checking, and it still says 103. It's a start.

I call Dylan. I miss him. I don't want to be stuck in this weird place. But his phone rings and rings and here's the answering machine: *"Hey, I'm not here so I'm probably writing some music or something. Leave me some words or don't, either one is cool."* The beep sounds and I sigh, hanging up, deciding against sounding like a sullen, dependent girlfriend.

I take a few deep breaths, trying to force myself to stop thinking about why Dylan isn't home, telling myself he isn't with Georgia.

I'm not quite sure how it happens, or maybe I am, and just can't find a good enough way to describe it. But here I am, sitting on the bathroom floor, cutting my arm with my blue shaving razor. The intense pain surprises me, but it starts to even out after a while, and then it's just a soothing, dull ache. I like the feeling.

I feel dizzy and light-headed and deliciously out of it. Which was kind of the point.

Chapter 6

Sunday brings its church bells and before-school blues. Shortly after I wake up, there's a knock on the door. "Dylan," I say, glad I'm wearing a sweatshirt.

"Hey, I have some awesome news!" He grins from ear to ear, pushing his hair away from his eyes. "We got a gig! I mean, it's nothing special, it's only our second, but it's a start, you know?"

"Aw, congrats!" I manage a smile. "When is it?"

"Tuesday night. It starts at eight. Can I count on you?"

"Of course," I say.

"Great." His face turns solemn. "So, um, did you call last night?"

"Yeah. It was no big deal."

"You sure?"

I hate when he stares at me like I'm a song he

can't figure out the lyrics to, no matter how hard he tries. My arm is burning, has been since last night. I pull my sweatshirt sleeves down over my hands. "Look, I was kind of upset and I just needed you. Seriously, it's fine."

He sighs, sitting down on the steps of my porch. "What happened, Raine?"

I weigh my options: talk to him, fall apart, never live it down. Or, go upstairs and study. "Look, I have a ton of work."

"Are you sure you can come to the show?"

I lean against the front door and close my eyes. "Don't act like I'm unsupportive."

"I'm not, I just —"

"I know," I say. "You want me to be there. So I'll be there."

"I want us to be *us* again," Dylan says. He takes a chance and kisses me, and I'm struck by how he still tastes the same.

"Me too. But it feels harder now. Like I'm always wondering what she's going to say to you at your next band practice. Or if she's going to try it again."

"Can we sit?" Dylan asks, motioning toward the white wicker bench on my front porch. Even though it's freezing, I nod. Once we're seated he says, "You know how shitty I feel about that, right? We're in the same band, sure, but that's it. She knows what's up. It won't happen again."

"I believe you," I say. And I do. Because when he leans forward and kisses me again, Dylan still tastes of promise. He sees the world the way I used to, the way I want to again. He sees it as something you can touch, like you can pull out the beauty and use it however you desire.

"Do you remember our first date?" he asks. "It was the middle of September and you kept saying how much you loved the leaves. You noticed everything, you know?"

"Fall air is my favourite smell," I say. "It's like cold air and fire."

He nods. "And you used to stand in the middle of the street, convinced you'd never get run over, and focus on the traffic lights like they were all that existed in the world." He tugs at the hole in his jean-clad knee. "I miss that girl."

"But I'm not her," I say. When he looks upset, I playfully hit his arm, my lame attempt at lightening up the moment. "Hey, people change."

"We don't have to." He stands up. "Are you doing anything right now?" I shake my head and he says, "Let's go somewhere."

So we get into Dylan's red car — he got a second-hand beige car and painted it his favourite colour — and he drives, Nirvana on the stereo. When we stop at a red light I focus on the way it melts into the sky, already dark with romance.

Dylan stops the car and we're at a park near my house known as "The Black Gate Park" because of its wrought iron gate. "Oh," I say, smiling. We came here all the time in tenth grade, him pushing me on the swings, us lying down in the grass, making out. It was all magical and wonderful. Jealousy fills me up; the beginning of our love was a bittersweet time. My dad was gone, and Dylan gave me something to look forward to every day, a reason to leave the house other than school.

"Do you think we can do this?" Dylan asks. "Move on?" He still looks at me with tender eyes as if he wants to wrap me up in a blanket so there could be hope for us yet.

"I think so," I say, and smile to prove it. We get out of the car and sit on a nearby bench, leaning our heads back and staring up at a sky that has seen it all, full of the world's secrets. We kiss furiously, like the good old days, and when we pull away my heart pounds. I haven't eaten in twelve hours. I figure I must be losing weight by the headaches. I feel incredibly alive.

**

I put two Band-Aids over my cut and pile on my usual bracelets before leaving the house. I hop on the subway, having agreed to meet everyone at the show. I don't expect anyone to notice my arm. And if they do, I doubt they would even know what to say. Cutting to them is a scene in a bad made-for-TV movie, an article in a magazine, a teen novel exploring life in a hospital. I am so far away from my friends, I'm starting to get used to the idea that we live on separate continents. Katrina's idea of misery is a TV character passed

out in her driveway after downing pills and te-
quila in Tijuana. Matt's concept of suffering is not
winning a football game or not scoring with a girl
at a party.

"Hey guys," I say, joining Katrina and Matt at a
little table. She's all dolled up in a black dress and
Uggs. Matt is wearing his blue and yellow football jersey with army pants.

"They are so ridiculous about carding here,"
Katrina greets me. She motions toward their
drinks. "How boring is it to still have to order
soda?"

I stick to a glass of water, thinking it'll help
cleanse my system, and decide to take my coat
off, even though I'm freezing. Everyone else has,
and I don't want to draw attention to myself.

Small talk fills the air until Dylan's band comes
on. Their music is on the grungy side — melodic
but loud. I am overwhelmed by how proud I am
of him as I watch them play. This is my boyfriend,
and look at how talented he is. I know the drum-
mer, Logan, because he's an old friend of Dylan's.
And then there is Georgia, dressed in skinny black
pants and a skimpy black t-shirt. She can't take
her eyes off Dylan. There is no way to miss it.
From the way she looks at him, you would definitely think they were a couple.

"Hey, what's up?" Katrina asks warmly. When
I shake my head she gives me a weak smile. "I
know. It's hard to see *her*, right?"

"Katrina," Matt says in a warning tone.

She rolls her eyes. "I know we said we wouldn't talk about it with Raine, but how can we not? Help me out here, Matt. I know Dylan's, like, your boy and all —"

"My boy?" Matt asks, laughing.

"We're just watching the end of life as we know it, that's all," Katrina says.

"Give him a break." My voice surprises all three of us. I clear my throat. "I don't agree with what he did, obviously. But we're working through it."

"Good for you!" Katrina says with a grin.

By the last song, I'm getting restless. The noise is too much, and it's too much looking at Dylan and Georgia. My head is pounding. My cut is burning, but I can't let it show.

"I'm going to the washroom," I announce, right as the set ends and the room erupts in applause. The bathroom is a single and is disgusting, which I should have expected in a seedy place like this. I go in and take a series of deep breaths before throwing cold water on my face.

I must be in there for a long time because there's a knock on the door. "Raine?" comes Dylan's voice, frantic and excited, but I can hear traces of disappointment, too. "Are you in there?" I feel frozen, unable to talk, and after a few seconds he sighs. "I can hear you. I'm coming in, okay?"

Dylan pushes the door open and closes it behind him, looking at me with raw, eager eyes. His hair is a total mess, his forehead's a little sweaty, and he's holding a bottle of water. He seems every

57

bit the gorgeous, cool musician, and I seem every bit his ugly, messed up girlfriend. I hate myself in this moment so much I almost can't stand it.

"Hi," I say, my voice wavering, like water is coming out instead of words. I left my coat at the table with Matt and Katrina, and I shiver in my bare sleeves, freezing.

"Hi," he repeats. "Are you okay? I didn't see you out there when we finished."

I nod, swallowing. "Yeah, I'm fine. Sorry, I was just getting really . . ." I shrug, realizing I can't explain. "I'm sorry. You guys were amazing though, really. Especially you."

"Thanks." This puts a big smile on Dylan's face. He is cloaked in happiness, but it doesn't last long. I can feel his eyes on my left arm even before I see him looking at it. I look down and see the two medium-sized Band-Aids on my arm have gotten wet, one of them peeling off to reveal the red sliver on my pale skin. My whole body goes numb. And time stops.

He walks over to me slowly and he puts his finger on the Band-Aid. When he looks at me, I feel the horror and the hurt and the disappointment in every inch of my body. "You can't do this," he says, as if that would make it better, make the cut go away faster. "You just . . . can't."

"Hey, you found it," I say, feeling my face harden like a clay mask. "Deal with the consequences."

"Fuck!" he yells. Shocked, I jump back slightly

58

from the sound of his voice. I'm so used to hearing him talk softly, in this slow gentle rhythm that I always believed was meant for me alone. This loud rock and roll argument feels horrible.

I put my hand over his. "It's fine, okay? I'm fine."

"Don't tell me you're fine," he says, "because I know it's a lie. But the way I feel about you? That's real. And so is your pain. It's so obvious that everyone can see it, including me." His eyes meet mine, and all the fireworks and sunsets are gone. Anger is the only reflection. "Especially me."

"But I'm fine," I say. I am a parrot, a tape recorder, an ongoing circle of excuses.

"How can you just tear yourself apart like this and expect me not to say anything? You never eat and sure, you do a pretty good job acting like you've got it all together, but I know that you don't."

When people say things like that, or even just address the problem, something happens to my mouth. It becomes sandpaper, dry and rough, and I can't speak. I can only stare at my boyfriend helplessly, a puppet hanging by a string, an elaborate spectacle.

Dylan's face changes, the fury twirling into hurt. "I feel like . . . there's this glass wall between us. Like even though you're right here with me, there's still this force that stops you from being able to see how much I love you."

"There is a wall," I say. "Its name is Georgia."

"If I wanted to be with Georgia, then I would be. But I don't. I want you."

"I'm sorry that I cut myself, and I'm sorry I keep hurting you, but I don't do it on purpose."

"You know what I think about before I go to bed every night?" Dylan asks. "I think about how we could stay together. I picture us doing that. I picture our kids. We'd have a boy and I'd teach him how to play guitar." He smiles, like he's remembering something that hasn't even happened yet — that might never happen. But it's a sad smile this time. His smile reminds me of so many things — fireflies, those old Victorian lampposts. I would be lucky to stay with him. Everyone probably thinks we will, too. They see us as the "perfect couple." When people say they don't want perfection, that it's unrealistic and that flaws are more beautiful, I think they're lying. Because when you research it, when you really look underneath it all, that's all anyone wants.

"I promised Logan I'd write some music after the show," Dylan says. "I'll call you later."

"Goodnight. I love you. I'm sorry." I give Dylan the words and he takes them, nodding.

But I don't tell him that I can't picture myself having kids. I don't tell him I can barely get myself through a whole day. I don't tell him the image I get when I picture a shared future: a grown-up Dylan with shorter hair but the same ripped jeans, me smoking in bed while he strums a guitar. But that's it. Just the two of us sitting on opposite sides of the bed, not talking.

I don't tell him I have only eaten an apple and some almonds since lunch. I don't tell him that when I skipped the cafeteria again to study in the library I ate half of a peanut butter and banana sandwich, then felt disgusted with myself and threw the rest away. I don't tell him that I'm already excited about morning coming, because I will get to wake up and start all over again. And this time, I won't eat anything at all.

I press my Band-Aids down a few times and swing the bathroom door open, facing a crowd that is drunk and happy, but all the faces become one big blur. It doesn't matter if I'm with a million people or just one, I'm still me.

"Can we go?" I ask Katrina, walking back to the table. "We can take the subway together."

"Sounds good to me," she says. She hugs Matt quickly before standing up. "See you later."

"Is everything cool?" Matt asks me, staring at me funny, and I nod, smoothing back my hair, hoping I don't look as awful as I feel.

Katrina's usual chatter fills the air as we head out into the cold. When we cross the street to get to the subway, I suddenly want to tell her about the fight. About the string of fights. As my best friend, she could help.

"You know, something happened tonight —" I start to say. Then Katrina's cell rings, the latest Lady Gaga single as her ring tone.

"Sorry, hold on," she says, grinning and flipping open her phone. "Adam! Hey!"

I stand next to her, listening to her tell him all about the show, watching the steady stream of people going in and out of the subway. Finally, she squeals, "See you soon!" and hangs up. "I'm heading over to Adam's," she says. "He's so great. Things are so great."

I force a smile, following her into the subway entrance. So much for confiding in my best friend.

* * *

Something happens to me now. I get worse.

The last week of term before the winter holidays, I skip the cafeteria every day, smoking cigarettes in the parking lot instead.

This is my life now: headaches so massive they push the definition, a real loathing for food, and protruding bones. I stand in front of the bathroom mirror at night, turning from side to side, critical as always. But I don't need food anymore. I start living on tiny snacks. I can live each day without needing anything at all.

I step on the bathroom scale: 100 pounds. Three digits suck, I've decided. I have got to be two digits.

Chapter 7

The last Friday of term passes in a whirl of school-work and anticipation for winter break. Katrina approaches me at my locker after the last bell, a big smile on her face.

"Someone named Katrina took her happy pills today," I say, putting the books from my afternoon classes away.

"Someone named Raine forgot," she frowns. "Can I talk to you? I've been thinking about something."

"Sure." I slam my locker shut. "Let's go sit outside on the front bench."

Once we're settled, Katrina takes a deep breath. "We're not really close anymore," she says. "And I really hate it."

I want to tell her that maybe she's part of the problem, that as soon as I was ready to tell her something important, she wasn't there for me.

So I tell her, but it comes out wrong. "Maybe if you spent less time with your pretty boyfriend, you'd have more time to be a friend," I say. "It's hard to talk to you sometimes, when all you care about is going to the mall and singing in that stupid musical."

"Wow," she says, shaking her head, wiping away a tear that falls onto her cheek.

I immediately regret it. "I'm sorry," I say, and then stop. There on the sidewalk right outside school is the guy from Starbucks. Andrew. He passes something to a boy and puts something else into his coat pocket. Strange; I didn't expect to see him again. I take him in — same black coat, but with baggy black pants and red Cons. The burst of colour is almost startling.

"Is it just me, or was that a drug deal?" Katrina asks.

Andrew glances in our direction and, after staring at me for a moment, grins and waves.

"Why does he know you?" she asks, our talk seemingly forgotten.

"Shhh," I say, smiling as Andrew approaches us.

"Hey," he says. "You go here?"

I nod. "Uh huh."

Katrina is staring at both of us, and I can practically see the wheels turning in her head. "Um, how do you two know each other?"

"Starbucks," Andrew says easily. "I'm Andrew. Who are you?"

She stares at him for a couple of seconds, as if deciding whether or not to respond. "Katrina. Nice to meet you."

Most guys react to Katrina by flirting — she is, after all, incredibly gorgeous. Andrew doesn't even seem to notice this, or if he does, he doesn't do anything about it.

"One of my friends goes to school here too," Andrew says. "I was just giving him a pack of cigarettes I owed him. He's throwing a party to-night." I realize how good-looking he really is, then feel my stomach start to hurt.

"A party," Katrina repeats, her blue eyes light-ing up.

Andrew nods, lighting a cigarette and offering me one. The hunger pains are starting up again, and a cigarette is the perfect thing to curb them. There's that word again — perfect. It sounds exactly like it is — the ideal thing, the ideal weight, the ideal person. I think that's comforting, because if I have learned anything recently, it is that things are not always as they seem. Every-thing and everyone is layered.

"It's at fifty-seven Charles Street West. It starts at eight. You should come." Andrew checks his phone and nods again. "I gotta go, but I hope to see you there."

He leaves, heading back over to his friend. I glance over at Katrina and notice she looks con-fused. "Look, I'm so sorry," I say. "I shouldn't have said those things. Why don't we go to the party? It could be fun, like old times."

"Okay. But how do you know him? How well do you know him? Because going to a party with some random guy is how you wind up on the news."

"Andrew's not like that," I say, and wonder how I know he's a good guy. But I have a feeling he is. "If it's boring, we can leave, okay?"

Katrina's eyes light up and I know she's herself again. "Cool. Let's go get ready."

***

The party is in a fancy apartment, but each party location is the same: anonymous and suddenly belonging to everyone. Andrew and I hang out in the kitchen, me sitting on the countertop while he rummages in the fridge. "You hungry?" he asks, pulling out a cardboard box full of pizza.

I shake my head, realizing that this is the first time I don't need an excuse. I like this, the same way I like how confident he is. It makes me feel more firmly rooted to the ground. Katrina is off flirting, so it has been just the two of us all night. I've found out a couple things about Andrew: he hates television; only watches movies; he's in his fourth year studying drama at U of T; he loves what he calls the "beautiful, painful desperation" of Bright Eyes and hates "happy music."

I'm finished my beer when Andrew's cell rings. I take another drag of my cigarette. He glances at me when he hangs up. "So I've got to go see this guy. You want to go for a ride?"

I think back to the scene Katrina and I witnessed outside school. It becomes suddenly obvious to me what this is, I've seen it enough in movies. "Are you bringing people drugs?" I ask flirtatiously.

"Why? You want some?" He smiles at me, holding out his hand. When I take it and hop down from the counter, I feel a little dizzy. Andrew laughs. "Drunk yet?"

"No," I say. I get drunk very easily, but not from one cup. I think about telling Katrina that we're leaving, but decide I can text her later.

I follow Andrew out of the house and into his car, an old black Toyota that needs a new paint job. But he doesn't seem to care about things like this.

"You didn't answer me," Andrew says, holding the door open so I can crawl into the passenger seat. He shuts it and walks over to the driver's side, getting in and starting up the engine.

"Yeah, I'm not really into drugs," I say, adjusting the rear-view mirror in front of me so I can see myself. Only the top of my face is visible, and this doesn't seem like enough. I want to be able to see it all. I sigh, tucking my hair behind one ear.

We turn the corner quickly. Andrew is a really fast driver. This doesn't seem dangerous though, just completely exciting. "Hey, that's cool. You're kinda innocent. I get that."

"I'm not innocent." He should see the scars on my arms, the ones inside of me.

He looks over at me, as if needing proof, and nods. "Alright."

This is all I need, this one word. It seems to say it all.

***

Christmas Eve, I ring Dylan's doorbell, shivering. The weather outside is below freezing, or ten thousand degrees below freezing if you want to be dramatic about it. When he called today to invite me to dinner, I accepted, mostly because I love Lauren, his mother. But then I immediately realized I can't get out of eating at a sit-down dinner.

Lauren opens the door and I get a whiff of her rose perfume and the turkey in the oven. My stomach rumbles at the smell. "Hi!" she says, hugging me tight, and then frowns. "Oh, you feel so cold! Come in, it's awful out there."

"Sorry I'm a bit late," I say, handing her my black coat, and pull my grey sweater tighter around me. I can never get warm these days.

"Hey Raine," Dylan says, coming out of the kitchen. We hug too, him kissing my forehead as we pull away.

"Why don't you two go sit down? Dinner's ready, so I'll bring everything in." Lauren grins, her teeth white like blank pages, and hurries into the kitchen.

Dylan and I sit across from each other. The table is round, not rectangular, so there's no awkward absence at one end. "How've you been?" he asks, and I wonder why he looks so nervous.

"Okay, I guess. How are you?"

"Katrina mentioned you went to a party? With some guy you met in Starbucks?"

I wince as I think of the hangover I had the next day, but can't help smiling at the mention of my new friend. "Yeah, Andrew. He's pretty cool."

"Um, okay, so . . ." Dylan begins, but Lauren comes in with the turkey, so big it needs its own house. She goes back into the kitchen and returns with potatoes, salad, and enough bread to feed an army. My boyfriend sighs, resigned to the fact that we are no longer alone. But I'm glad.

I need to figure out an excuse.

Saying I'm hungry won't work because I've already used that to death, and it's obvious I haven't eaten dinner yet. Then the perfect excuse dawns on me.

"Oh, I'm a vegetarian," I tell Lauren. "I can't have the turkey."

"I forgot," Dylan says sheepishly. "Sorry, Mom."

"Do you want me to make you something else?" Lauren looks concerned.

I shake my head, content with the idea of vegetables. I hate potatoes, but I could eat one and throw it up later. That's the best solution: that way everyone's happy — it'll look like I've eaten, but I'll still get it out of my system. "No, thank you," I say.

Lauren nods and the three of us start passing the dishes around, serving ourselves. I take a big helping of salad, a piece of bread, and the smallest potato on the plate. It still seems massive to me.

"So are you enjoying your winter vacation?" Lauren asks me between mouthfuls of salad and bread. Seeing people eat never fails to make me uncomfortable.

"No," I say with a short laugh. "I love school too much."

Dylan laughs too, shoving a big slice of turkey into his mouth. It annoys me when other people eat a lot. I am utterly convinced that just from staring at it, food is magically being ingested by my body.

Lauren's laugh is tinkly, like an acoustic guitar. She is definitely a very cool adult. I'm jealous of Dylan, of the way the two of them live, like friends almost.

I force myself to eat half a slice of bread, then the potato. I wonder if my smile looks real; I can't even tell by the way it feels anymore. Suddenly the dining room lights seem too bright and my stomach is burning and everything is just too much. I cough, trying to calm myself down. Why can't I be normal? Just for one single night? Girlfriends are supposed to eat the freaking turkey. They're supposed to *eat*, period.

"Aren't you hungry?" Dylan asks. "You've barely eaten anything."

"I ate lots!" I say. I can't be rude in front of his mom, and he knows that.

Lauren stares at the two of us, worried. I'm afraid now, of this moment, of this holiday. "Okay," he says quietly.

***

After dinner, I help Lauren put the dishes away while Dylan goes upstairs to call one of his band-mates. I worry he's calling Georgia.

"You're looking a little thin these days," Lauren says. "Is everything alright?"

"Oh yeah," I say immediately, expecting her to take my word for it. But I can tell from her expression she's not finished.

"You remind me of a girl I knew in high school," she says in a voice smooth like honey.

"I do?" I lean against the counter.

She nods slowly. "Yeah. She was beautiful the same way that you are — striking, but not flashy. She had no idea how gorgeous she was. She was really troubled. She cared too much about how others saw her, and that ruined so many of her teenage years." Lauren pauses and I know what's coming next before she even says it. "She was anorexic. She hid behind baggy clothes and too much makeup and gallons of coffee. But that made her beauty go — slowly at first, and then much quicker. God, it was heartbreaking, watching that. It was like she got . . . drained of everything she was, until there wasn't much left."

Oh my God, I think. *She knows*. Did Dylan tell

her, or does she see it, the way you'd notice someone's new haircut or purple eyeliner? "Did she ... get better?" I ask, aware of how shaky my voice sounds, the noise the sky makes before a storm.

"She . . . she died," Lauren says, tears forming in her brown eyes. "We all tried to help her, but we couldn't reach her, no matter what we did. She was so far away, even if she was sitting right in front of us."

I cover up my surprise and compose myself enough to ask another question: "How old was she?"

"Seventeen. You must think it's strange, me standing here and telling you all these morbid things, but . . . high school is so hard, you know? It's all about appearances and what's on the outside. Girls like my friend . . . they had so many terrible things going on inside, but they never found a way to let them out."

For a fleeting moment, I see myself in that girl's position. I'm as old as she was, after all. I see myself getting thinner and thinner, the pounds rapidly slipping off until I'm bonier than I ever dreamed, and I see myself crash. Everyone is sad at my funeral, which isn't rare, of course, because that's what people do. But then I see Dylan sobbing, and it scares me.

Without even realizing it at first, I start to cry.

Lauren reaches over to give me a hug, and I hold on as tight as I can, my fear obvious but silent between the two of us.

But I still feel the potato like a brick in my

stomach. I smile weakly at Lauren and head for the upstairs bathroom. As I lean by the toilet and stick my fingers down my throat, it's not me. I'm watching someone else do this, a lonely girl, not me but someone else.

I flush the toilet, coughing horribly, and I hear a loud sound from the hallway. Shit. Did someone hear?

I am met by Dylan's stricken face when I open the bathroom door. "Okay, now you're scaring me," he says. He looks like he wants to say more but can't find the words, the alphabet jumbled up in his head. I relate to that. I feel jumbled, too.

"Dylan . . ." I begin, unsure of where I'm going with this.

"Don't try to sweet-talk your way out of this. What was the point of eating the little bit that you did?"

"The point," I say sharply, "was to look *normal* in front of your mom."

"It's Christmas! Why does everything have to be such a big deal?" Dylan is on a roll. "You want to lose more weight, don't you? You want to just waste away until there's nothing even left of the person I love? You want to —"

"Stop it!" I interrupt.

"Why?"

"Because you're breaking my heart. I'm sorry I can't be the perfect girlfriend who can eat a massive Christmas dinner, but I can't do it. Thank your mom for me. I have to go."

Dylan follows me downstairs and watches as I tug on my coat. "I guess things are really bad now," he says.

I shrug. "I guess so."

Chapter 8

In the days after Christmas, I hang out with Andrew. There is something about him that's unlike anyone else I know. He seems to get all the unspoken stuff. Pain is a language, and Andrew seems to be fluent. Dylan and I haven't spoken since the disaster that was Christmas dinner. New Year's Eve, I'm home alone, ignoring the so-called holiday that seems pretty silly to me. Andrew calls and asks if I want to come over. He says he'll leave the door unlocked, so I should just walk in.

Which I do. And I walk into a world unlike the decorative pillows and fancy paintings of my house. Andrew lives in a loft in the Annex, home of poets and actors and artists — basically, my idea of heaven. The floors are grey and concrete, the walls painted bright green, a brick wall near the spiral staircase. Most of the furniture in the open kitchen/living room is metal, and it is incredibly messy, newspapers and coffee cups littering the floor, cigarette butts on the countertop. There is an upstairs part with two bedrooms, and from where I'm standing, they look messy too.

Andrew is sitting on the floor smoking a joint when I arrive. Leaning against the brick wall, his knees brought up to his chest, he reminds me of a painting. Something beautiful to look at; something you admire and need to figure out. I am struck by the realization that there is a lot to figure out.

"Hey," he says, motioning for me to sit beside him. He offers me the joint, and when I shake my head, he nods and brings it up to his lips again.

It isn't the drugs themselves that scare me, or the altered state your mind goes into, the universes to which you travel. I am afraid — deathly afraid — of the "munchies" that weed produces, the sudden need to just eat and eat and eat.

"So I auditioned for this indie film today and I got a callback," Andrew says, breaking into my thoughts.

"That's amazing," I say. "What part did you read for?"

"Someone's depressed boyfriend. Which is a role I sure have played in real life, so I guess it makes sense."

I nod. "Well they do say that art imitates life."

Andrew is quiet and stubs out his joint on the concrete floor. When he answers, he keeps his eyes downward, the first time I have seen him look vulnerable. "I was sixteen when I . . . tried to kill myself." He rolls up the sleeve of his grey sweatshirt, revealing the dark crimson scar on the inside of his left forearm. "Pretty stupid, huh? I became a statistic, just another teenager who cut the wrong way. My girlfriend freaked."

"Did you think maybe it was a sign?" I ask. "Something out there telling you that you still had more to accomplish?"

"I can't really do that glass-half-full shit," he says.

"Me either. So . . . you had a girlfriend at the time?"

"Yeah. She thought if I loved her more, I would have wanted to stay."

"But it's not always about other people," I say quickly, unable to stop the words from rolling out before it gets too personal. "Maybe it has nothing to do with them. It's about . . . you. And about making sense of your pain, whichever path you choose."

Now Andrew is the one who looks impressed. "Yeah. Exactly. How do you know that?"

I shrug, attempting to imitate his casualness. "I think we speak the same language. I never tried suicide, but . . ."

"But you know what it's like to think about it?"

"Yeah," I say. Sometimes it seems like the simplest solution, the best way to never have to think about food again, or how much I want to weigh, or how much I miss my dad. Sometimes I wonder what there is to live for, especially when Dylan and I keep tearing our relationship apart. "I hope you get the part," I add lamely.

Andrew doesn't answer, just stares at me for a moment, as if seeing some new crack in my face or a shade of colour I hadn't noticed. "You have a story," he says. "Everyone does, but I think you especially do." He pauses, then continues, "I think you're sad." Something passes between us, and he nods, realizing stories can't begin unless a person is willing to tell them.

"Where's your bathroom?" I ask, and he points to a door near the kitchen. Once inside, I'm met with my reflection: my straight hair, my dark green dress, the gold bangles on my right wrist. I stare at the hollowness that has begun to inch its way into my cheeks, wondering if it has been there all along. I wonder what Andrew sees when he looks at me; if he can see the foggy clouds of indecision that I deal with each day.

When I step out of the washroom, Andrew is talking on his cell phone and laughing hysterically, so I know the drugs have kicked in. When he hangs up, I say, "It's after midnight. I think I should go."

"Stay over," he says, so easily.

"Where would I sleep?" I ask. His photographer roommate, Sascha, has been in Boston for the past week on an assignment for a magazine. I don't know much about her, just that she and

Andrew have been friends most of their lives, and she's a few years older than his twenty-one.

"My bed," he says. I must look as surprised as I feel because he laughs. "Come on. It's no big deal. We can just sleep."

"Okay," I say.

"You want to crash now or hang out a little more?"

"No, I'm okay. I'll stay up." My eyes are closing already, but I don't want to pass up the chance to talk to him. We both settle onto the couch.

Andrew looks at me with a smirk, cheeky yet charming. "So what's your family like? We haven't covered that ground yet."

"I don't have any siblings. My mother is a total workaholic. I mean, it's like pushing the definition of the word. And, as for my dad . . ." Here comes the hard part, I think, aware of the way my chest seems to tighten. "He died when I was fifteen."

Each time I say this out loud, it feels like losing him all over again.

"Oh, man," Andrew says, the usual sympathetic look creeping across his features, but not as annoying because I think he must mean it. "That's tough."

"Thanks for not saying you're sorry," I tell him. "That's what people always say. I know it's sad news to hear, but it's just way too cliché."

"Well, in case you haven't noticed," he reaches over to put his hand over mine, "I'm not exactly a cliché kind of guy."

For a few moments all I can focus on is the warmth of his hand, the butterflies that spread throughout me, making it hard for me to breathe. I think of the shivers I used to get when Dylan and I first started dating, when we were still learning the ways in which we could fit together.

I pull my hand away. "Andrew . . ."

He sighs. "I know, I know, you've got a boyfriend. But I think you're pretty. Sue me." He stands up, stretching his arms out above his head, his t-shirt inching up and revealing a sliver of his stomach. "Let's sleep."

I follow him upstairs and we get into bed, me on the left and him on the right. I lie on my side away from him, attempting sleep. All I can think about is the fact that Andrew called me beautiful. Something must be working, I think. I only ate a banana for breakfast and a small yogurt for lunch, I can afford to eat breakfast the next morning.

My stomach rumbles as if on cue, and maybe it is, waiting for the right instant to make its music. I fall asleep listening to the cars rolling by outside with a terrible pain in my chest.

Chapter 9

The first Friday of the new term brings a school dance. Even though I'm against the so-called rituals that the world believes you must experience in order to be a fully evolved person, I agree to go. It's partly as a favour to Katrina, who loves school activities, and partly to spend time with Dylan. I prepare all week, eating only two things each day: a rice cake with the tiniest bit of peanut butter and one apple. It works, too. The night of the dance, I step onto the scale in my black bra and underwear and grin at the number: 95.

There is room for improvement, of course, but this means tonight will be perfect.

I smooth dark silver onto my eyelids before grinning at my reflection. My strapless black dress fits perfectly. I can do this; I can lose what I want. This kind of power is incredible. I take a sip of my Nescafé and decide to paint my nails black, if only to instill a little anti-conformity into the evening.

The doorbell rings, and I admire my wavy hair. I look glamorous, more sophisticated. Shock covers Dylan's face when I open the door, and I force a smile and ask, "Is that good or bad?"

"C'mere," he says, pulling me to the side of the porch. "What happened? You look pretty, yeah, but you are so bony!"

I try not to smile. That would not go over well. "Everything's cool," I say. "Let's go, okay?"

We join Katrina and Matt in the backseat of the limo Dylan rented. I stumble a bit in the black heels I borrowed from my mother, but that could be because they are a little big. "Looking good," Matt says, and I wonder if he means it.

"You too," I say. What is it about suits that make guys seem like little boys playing lawyers and big ad executives?

"Isn't this, like, the coolest thing?" Katrina asks, gesturing around her.

"I'm practical," Dylan tells her. "We needed transportation. I took care of it."

"No, you are a big softie and you know it," she says. "Now come on! It's time to party!"

Dylan pins a corsage to my dress — a simple white flower — and as he does so, his hand brushes my collarbone. I wince without thinking, because it hurts, and when his eyes question this I shake my head. "That's pretty," I say.

We pick up Adam on the way to the hall. Katrina

leaves the limo door open and I peer out, watching as he swoops her up into a giant hug and then leans down to kiss her. The two of them start furiously making out, probably forgetting we can see.

"He did not just grab her ass," Matt says.

"Jealous much?" I ask.

"I just don't like the guy."

"Yeah, well, *you* don't have to date him." Dylan hits Matt lightly in the arm.

Finally, we're on our way again, but I can't stop the heady feeling I get when we arrive at the hall. I feel completely exhausted, but I tell myself I just need water and focus on the couples lining up to have their pictures taken next to a giant circular staircase. The place is elegant, with dozens of small tables decorated with beige tablecloths and white rose centrepieces.

"Let's go take our picture," Dylan says, putting his arm around me, and I don't object. As he puts his arms around me, I feel like we're a normal couple.

"Smile," says the photographer.

And I give an ear-splitting grin, wanting so badly for this moment to last forever.

"That was good," the photographer tells us, and Dylan kisses my cheek.

Half an hour later, as we all wait for dinner to be served, I cannot hide how faint I feel. Sitting down seems to just make it worse, and I grab Dylan's arm and stand up. "Let's dance."

"We're going to eat," he says coldly.

I lean closer and kiss his neck, and he smiles at our friends. "Or, uh, we're going to dance. See you guys later."

I exchange a smile with Katrina and take Dylan's hand, blinking a few times, wanting the room to stop spinning. Alphaville's "Forever Young" is playing, which seems both depressing and hauntingly pretty. "*Let's dance in style, let's dance for a while*," Dylan whispers in my ear, pulling me into an embrace. I am overcome with so much intense, insane love for him. How is it possible to love another human being this much? I close my eyes and lean my head on his shoulder. But of course I'm not allowed such a pure, stunning moment. Of course it has to be ruined. My head is too heavy to hold up, and I feel tears spilling out of my eyes as I stop moving, trying to smile, trying not to make Dylan worry.

"I'll be right back," I say, searching for the washroom. I need to lean against something solid. I stare in the mirror at my washed-out skin and wonder why I look so grey. I mean, yes, I've been living on rice cakes and apples. But my body should be used to this.

A group of girls stumble into the washroom, dressed in identical beige dresses, the three of them laughing drunkenly. I take this as my cue to leave, and I step back out into the hall, realizing that, for real this time, *the entire room is spinning.*

I spot Matt out of the corner of my eye, walking toward me. "Hey!" he shouts. "They just served this amazing chicken —" My eyes start fluttering, my chest feels weird, and I try to smile but I can't. "Raine?" he asks. My eyes close and I hear his voice getting softer and softer, a blanket of noise covering my body. I hear other voices too, and as I hit the floor I see my shoes, my borrowed heels that my mother never even noticed that I took.

***

It is like you are a painting, and every time you skip a meal the colours dissolve, and then you wake up one morning and you are not quite the masterpiece that you anticipated. You are ugly.

***

I open my eyes and find myself in a hospital. The entire room is white, but instead of calming me down, it makes me feel incredibly anxious.

My mother is sitting on a chair near my bed. She reaches over and puts her hand on mine. "Good, you're awake," she says.

"What the hell am I doing here?" I ask, suddenly realizing how sore my throat is. My dress is draped across the chair and I'm in an uncomfortable white paper gown.

"You fainted last night," she says, her voice soft for a moment. "At the dance. Matt told the teachers on duty and they called an ambulance. I got here as fast as I could."

I rub my eyes, my fingers becoming smudged with silver eyeliner. "I don't need to be here," I say. I realize my left arm is hooked up to a tube. Intravenous. Right. This is unnecessary.

I try to sit up, just as the door swings open. In walks a doctor, dressed typically in beige pants and a big white overcoat, pens clipped into the pocket. His hair is orange. "Hi," he says, and from the smile he gives my mother I can tell they've been talking. "I'm Dr. Shelbourn. How are we feeling?"

"We?" I ask, hating him immediately. Obviously I'm the only one lying in this hospital bed. I bet he's feeling just peachy.

"You had a bit of a scare there," he says. Then he turns to my mother. "Would you mind giving us a minute or two to talk?"

"I don't need to talk," I say, as my mother nods and slips out of the room.

Dr. Shelbourn walks closer to the bed and smiles faintly. "I know this must be scary. But I'd like to ask you a few questions."

"I don't see why."

"You don't think there's any reason your mother might be worried, or that there's anything we could discuss?"

He's not being rude. I can see that. He actually wants me to answer. So I say, "I was at a dance. It was fun, and then it wasn't. Now I'm here."

"Look, Raine, this will be a lot easier if you answer these questions as honestly as you can." He pulls a notepad and pen out of his jacket pocket — the stereotypical doctor, ready to heal. "How would you describe your eating habits? Do you eat three meals a day, or do you eat a few small meals? Or one bigger meal?"

"It depends," I say.

"On what?"

"On different things." I rub my eyes. "I'm tired. Can we stop now?"

"One more question," Dr. Shelbourn says. "Your mother mentioned you were at the dance with your boyfriend and friends. How do they feel about your eating disorder?"

"Well," I say, "that isn't relevant, considering I don't have one."

He nods. He goes into the hallway and returns a few minutes later with my mother, then addresses both of us. "It would be best if we could get Raine into a treatment program right away," he says, "but unfortunately there is a waiting list." They exchange a grimace and he continues, "Typically we would admit a patient into our clinic, or they could come in for outpatient therapy and visit our nutritionist. I'd suggest putting your name down on the waiting list and coming in for outpatient therapy in the meantime."

"There's no need," I say.

"How long would the wait be?" my mother asks.

"We have a patient who is nearing recovery and has met all of her goals. It should be a month at the most," Dr. Shelbourn replies.

I close my eyes and grit my teeth. Who is he to decide this? It's my life, can't I live it the way I choose? I don't want to talk to anyone. I don't want to be here. And I don't want to come back.

"Don't worry," Dr. Shelbourn tells me, offering what he probably thinks is a comforting smile. "You will be in good hands. There are other girls in the program, and patients find it's a very supportive environment."

The fact that he's trying to get me to like him, to feel that he understands me, is the most ridiculous part of this whole thing. I'm not like other girls, and he can't just assume my life will fit into the same box as the rest of them.

"Well, let's get you home, then," my mom says. "I'll leave you to change."

The two of them chat as they walk into the hallway. I slip back into my fancy dress, feeling like my heart is beating ten times the normal rate. What am I going to do? I cannot and will not be stuck in a place that forces me to eat and forces me to talk about my so-called problems. It's just not an option.

How can it be an option when I have everything under control?

Chapter 10

I am standing in a room of mirrors. Hundreds of mirrors. I can't escape, I can't pretend I'm pretty, because it's all there: my fat thighs, my huge stomach, my disgusting body. Everything is there.

It's a nightmare, I realize, sitting up in bed. Head pounding, heart racing.

It's four in the morning, only five hours until school begins. It strikes me, suddenly, that I don't want to go back. Just what is waiting for me? A few more weeks of headaches and homework before my mother drags me into a clinic?

I push the worry out of my mind and read until pale yellow light dances on my bedroom walls. With an hour left, I dress in jeans and a big grey sweater and go downstairs to make coffee to put into a canteen. Caffeine is what I am living on. Last night my mother tried to enforce the "meal plan" Dr. Shelbourn suggested by leaving dinner on my desk, and I flushed it down the toilet while she was watching TV with Ben.

Dylan is waiting for me on a bench outside school.

"Hey," he says, leaning over to kiss me when I sit down next to him. "How are you doing?"

I know the answer he's looking for, but I'm not going to give it to him.

He motions toward my silver canteen. "Is that breakfast?"

I start to stand but he stops me, touching my hand, and it makes me so sad. He is so warm and I am so cold. How is this ever going to work out?

"Raine, you just *fainted* at a dance! You were in the hospital! You have to talk to me."

The bell rings, giving us three minutes to get to class, because that is really just so important.

I start walking in the direction of home. Dylan calls my name. Shouts it, actually. But for the first time, I don't care to listen to what he has to say.

***

I sleep all day. When I wake up, my house is still empty, but the silence is loud. Then I hear the front door being unlocked and my mother's heels dancing across the wooden floor. I close my eyes, wanting to go back to sleep, not wanting to think. But the sound of her heels comes closer and she knocks on my door. Not waiting for an answer, she comes right in.

"We need to talk," she says, leaning against the doorframe. "The school called me and said you skipped all of your classes today."

"That would be correct."

"Can you please sit up? This is serious. I don't know what to do anymore."

I could sit up, I guess, but my body feels like it weighs a million tons. I close my eyes again.

"Sometimes I think it would be better for all of us if you lived somewhere else for a while," she says. "I'm this close to calling your Aunt Louise to ask if she wouldn't mind if you stayed there."

"So call her," I say, rolling my eyes and turning over onto my side, away from her. She can do whatever she wants, it doesn't mean I have to go.

My mother sighs. "You're not in the mood to talk. Alright. I will check in on you later and we can continue this conversation."

I must have fallen back asleep because when my eyes open, my bedroom is filled with sunlight. My phone says ten AM.

My mother and Ben are at work. That is all I can focus on. I grab my black suitcase and throw every article of clothing I own into it, along with my favourite books, and put my MacBook into my black messenger bag. Then I text Andrew. He replies immediately with one word: *yes*.

I write a note and leave it on my mother's bed: *"I'm fine. I'm going to live with a friend for a while. Don't contact me. I'll call if I'm ready."*

I write this note to be a good person, a good

daughter. But it's not like she really cares. She was "this close" to sending me away herself.

He hugs me as soon as he answers his door. We both sink onto the couch and he opens a bottle of cheap champagne. He lights a cigarette and tosses me one. I feel very bohemian and full of an independence I only dreamed about before.

"Thanks," I say, staring at the cigarette in my hand. "I didn't know where else to go."

"It's cool." Andrew gently touches my hair, pushing my sweater off my shoulder. I feel shivers in every part of my body. When he looks at me, I know what's going to happen. He leans closer and his lips are on mine, just as passionate as the rest of him is. I almost cannot believe it's finally happening, everything that has been in the back of my mind for a while now.

"You must . . . you must know how much I want this," he says, his voice low, kissing my neck. And I want it too. I nod, and I don't feel any hesitation when we end up making out. All I feel, really, is the complete intoxication of the moment.

We don't bother to go upstairs. Having sex with a twenty-one-year-old boy on a couch in his grungy artistic loft makes me feel more grown-up than ever. He is skinny. I find beauty in this, in his shoulder blades, the bones of his wrists. Our pale skin matches, and I feel my breath catch in my throat.

"You have a great body," he says, afterwards, passing me a cigarette. He smiles as he runs his hand over my stomach.

I know I don't, but today I feel that maybe I look alright. "You definitely do," I say. I lean over to kiss him, thinking *who is this girl?*

She's me. And I seem to grow more and more into her each day, trying on her smiles, her clothes, her mannerisms. Finding that we are similar after all.

Chapter 11

"You aren't going back, are you?"

The question wakes me up. I've been at Andrew's for a few days now. I glance over and see Andrew lying on his side in bed beside me. "High school's rough, there's nothing wrong with taking some time off," he says. "I considered not going to university, but knew I'd probably drink myself into oblivion every single day. I wanted something to anchor me."

I have something to anchor me too, I think, and smile as my stomach rumbles.

"Parents are ridiculous. They act like they know everything about you. I ignore mine most of the time. My dad's a banker and my mom is one of those socialites. They think acting is stupid and that I'm never going to make it. But how am I supposed to tell them that I don't even know if an actor is what I want to be? How do you tell your parents that the only thing keeping you going is that one day you might possibly be happy?" He shakes his head, frowning. "And I can't tell them that it doesn't seem likely."

This is such a tender, raw moment, and I feel for Andrew in every part of my body. "You pretty much read my mind," I say. "But replace actor with writer."

"Yeah? That's cool. I try to write but most of it is complete shit."

"Well, it can be hard to find the right words, despite how corny that sounds."

Andrew laughs. "You seem to have no trouble with words. Everything you say fits pretty well."

"You'd be surprised," I say, then think, maybe not. Maybe he'd get it. Maybe he would be able to understand that I would rather starve than speak.

"How did you decide on drama?" I ask, wanting to know as much as I can about him.

He shrugs, approaching this question with the same careless attitude he applies to everything, but it's a passionate nonchalance. "It happened accidentally . . . I signed up for drama in grade nine thinking it would be an easy course to snooze through, but in grade eleven I got serious. It seemed natural to major in it. Now I'm playing the male lead in *Romeo and Juliet* at school, so it worked out."

"So cool," I say, just as my cell phone buzzes. It's Katrina. Again. When I don't answer she leaves a message, and I listen with gritted teeth:

"What's up? Why aren't you in school? Everyone is freaking out. Please call me! Or call Dylan! Call someone!"

Dylan.

I double over, a sharp pain in my stomach. I just cheated on my boyfriend.

How did this slip my mind?

I know. Of course I know. Something is connecting Andrew and me to each other, some invisible tightrope I have chosen to walk across. I don't regret it, either. But I can't ignore the consequences.

"I have to deal with something," I say, standing up. I dress quickly and descend the spiral staircase, slipping into the tiny washroom and dialing digits I have long since committed to memory. Numbers I probably will not dial again in the near future.

***

I wait at a nearby Starbucks with my hands wrapped around a paper cup. It's four o'clock when Dylan walks in. Andrew is in class. I planned it that way.

"So," he says, skipping the hello and swimming right into the moment. "It's weird to see you at a different Starbucks. You were so attached to the one in your neighbourhood." He takes a deep breath and pushes his hair off his forehead. I want to be the one mussing up his beautiful hair. I want to touch him, but I know I can't. Something has shifted between us. "So what's the deal? Are you really willing to skip school, leave home, ignore all your friends, all for this guy?" He steps closer. "Are you really letting me go?"

"Yes." I speak with more confidence than I feel, needing to be in control, when I can feel my heart slipping away and going in another direction. "I'm sorry, Dylan. But . . . I can't do the fights anymore. I need a new start."

He sighs, sadness spreading like water across his face. "This isn't the way it was supposed to be. We were supposed to go to university together and be that couple that managed to stay so in love through everything."

"People break up," I say. "It's not a big deal."

Dylan shakes his head, laughing meanly. "All you do is cover up how you're feeling and hope no one figures it out. But I know you, and we all know what's going on. Have fun with your new boyfriend."

He leaves.

I see this as if I were watching a movie, a dramatic scene playing across my eyes, two hearts breaking at the same time. I reach up to touch my cheek. Dry.

***

I decide to dye my hair. A rainbow of bottles face me at the nearest convenience store. I pick up a bottle of pale yellow dye and turn it over, reading

97

the instructions. Considering it. Becoming blond would definitely be a big change. I wouldn't even look like myself. I pick up some peroxide, too.

Andrew is running lines when I get back to the loft. He's pacing the room wearing only boxers, mumbling to himself and looking frustrated.

"You look so adorable," I say, closing the door behind me and smiling at him. "Like this serious actor."

He walks over and kisses me. "The only thing I'm serious about is that I suck at memorization. And come on, we both know you're the only adorable one around here."

I shake my head. "Am not."

"Are so."

"What are we, four?"

"I'm three. You're four." Andrew grins. "So what's in the bag?"

"Hair dye," I tell him. "Do you think you could help me? I have no idea what I'm doing."

Andrew takes the bag from my hand and heads toward the bathroom. "Let's make you even more beautiful."

I follow him, tensing up at his comment. After the peroxide is on, he spreads on the pale goo.

"I guess if we screw up I can just go back to black," I say, reaching up to scratch my scalp.

Andrew gently brings my hand down to the counter. "Don't touch. We won't screw up. I've dyed my hair millions of times."

"Oh yeah?"

"First, green when I was thirteen which didn't go over well with my parents, but I thought I was such a badass. Then I dyed it blue, then red, then blond because I was fifteen and thought I'd get girls that way."

"Why'd you switch back to black again?" I ask.

He pauses for a second, an indication that the answer is important. "You know that girlfriend I was talking about? She liked it black the best. She said the other colours were a way of hiding, that I should just 'embrace who I am and screw anyone who disagrees.'" I can hear the hurt in his voice.

"That's sweet. Sounds like you still think about her a lot."

His eyes meet mine in the mirror. "Well, you never do forget your first love. Maybe you never get over it, I have no clue. I'm over her, but . . ."

"You'll save a small piece of your heart for her?" I immediately think of Dylan, and how a piece seems far too insignificant for everything he has meant to me.

Andrew laughs. "Yeah, something like that. Wow, that was such a Hallmark card. So, time to wait while this works. Do you want some coffee?"

"What a question."

"Right. I'll be back in a sec."

When it's finally done, Andrew runs a brush through my hair, looking pleased. I stare at my reflection. It's like he created this new girl that I see in front of me. Or maybe she has been here all along, waiting for the right moment to show herself.

"Maybe this was a way of hiding," Andrew says, resting his hands on my shoulders, "but at least you're hiding with me."

***

I get a job. My first day at Fresh, a vegetarian restaurant in the neighbourhood, is hectic. I like the fast pace, since my daily weigh-ins show I'm not losing as much weight as I want. My scale is tucked away in one of the bathroom drawers. I figure Andrew was thinking more along the lines of dental floss and deodorant when he offered me a drawer, and I get a small thrill at keeping this secret. This is still mine.

The first few hours, I'm afraid of dropping a plate or forgetting an order. But soon I feel more comfortable and realize I can do this.

"Hey, you're doing great," another waitress, Sarah, says to me as she grabs a salad from the kitchen area. "Most people can barely keep up when they start out."

I smile, proud of myself. I hadn't expected to be good at this, but then again, I hadn't expected a lot of the things that have occurred.

***

"Hey, Andrew, I got you your favourite," I say, entering the loft after work with two cups from a café down the street. "I don't know how you stomach banana lattes. They sound gross." It isn't until I've shut and locked the door behind me that I realize Andrew isn't here, but a girl with short red hair and a camera around her neck is staring at me. More like glaring, actually. "Oh. You must be Sascha."

Sascha nods, unfazed, still looking at me. She is dressed in a ripped denim skirt and a black tank top. She is about average size — not skinny, but not fat either. Her gaze makes me feel uncomfortable, almost like she's a mirror, showing what there is to both like and dislike about myself. "You must be the new roommate," she says.

I stand awkwardly, unsure of what to say. I sip my black coffee just to have something to do.

"Whoa, you are way skinny," she says, her tone cold.

Andrew is coming down the spiral staircase, smiling at her. "Don't bug Raine." He walks over to me and takes the latte that I hand him. "Thanks, you're the best. How'd the new job go?" The smile he flashes me is like the glint of gold bangles.

"Really well, actually." I return the smile.

"She's working at Fresh," Andrew tells Sascha, taking a long sip of his drink.

She nods, unsmiling. "You guys seem awfully chummy."

"We're more than chummy," he says, putting his arm around my waist. He turns to me. "Don't mind her. She gets weird about new people. She's got a problem with change."

Sascha rolls her eyes. "Sweetheart, lay off the pills. I gotta go. I've got another wedding job. Lame-o."

When she's gone, the sound of the door closing echoing throughout the loft, I look over at Andrew. "She hates me."

"She doesn't know you. She's like an over-protective big sister."

I sigh, holding my coffee cup with two hands, letting it warm me up. "Great. This is going to be tons of fun."

"Sarcasm is unattractive." He grins, a mocking tone to his voice. "Don't you hate when people say stuff like that?"

"Hell yeah. My mom talks like that. It's exhausting." I realize it doesn't matter that I'm not living at home anymore, I have the same amount of contact with my mom either way.

Andrew sits on the couch and motions for me to join him. When I do, he puts his hand over mine. "Can I ask you something?" I nod and he continues. "Why are you so skinny?"

I always freeze at the mention of food or my weight. "I'm not that skinny," I say.

"You eat healthy, right? You work at Fresh, and you're a vegetarian." He sounds uneasy, but then his confidence returns. "I don't think I could do that, not eating meat. Never say never, but I'm not in a rush to try it."

"It's easier," I say. He nods, finishing his drink and leaning over to kiss me. I realize this

— whatever it is between us — is so much easier, too.

**

"Can I bum one?" Sascha asks, coming down the stairs, tying a white scarf through her hair. It's the last Saturday of January, and I've been curled up on the couch all morning working on a poem. She takes the cigarette I hand her and uses a black lighter from her red coat. "Thanks. How's it going?"

"Okay, I guess."

She nods, sitting in the green beanbag chair next to the couch. "We got off on the wrong foot. I apologize for that. But you seem cool and Andrew seems to like you."

"Thanks," I say.

The toilet flushes and Andrew comes out of the washroom, looking wild and frantic. "What's wrong with you?" Sascha asks him.

He doesn't answer, doesn't even look at her. He just starts pulling out the couch cushions, looking for something. He throws a bunch of magazines on the coffee table to the floor, then heads toward the bookcases.

"Did you lose something?" I ask, and when Sascha glares at me I shrug. "It's a logical question."

"Andrew, sweetheart, stop it," she says, walking over and putting her arm around his shoulder. "You know it's not good for you."

"Where the fuck are my pills?" He pushes her away harshly. I notice the bags underneath his eyes and how incredibly pale he looks.

"Don't be mad," she says softly, "but I threw them out. I just . . . I thought you should stop. Try to be without them for a few days."

Andrew is shaking his head, running a hand through his hair. "Don't you fucking understand?" She tries to put her hand on his arm and he throws it off him. "No, don't touch me. I'm gonna go." He grabs his keys from the kitchen counter and heads out of the loft, slamming the door.

"What the hell was that?" I ask Sascha, feeling shaky and a little scared.

"He's a complete addict," she says, and then smiles at me weakly. "He's got a problem."

I nod, a headache coming on. "What does he take?"

"Sleeping pills," she says. "He's been doing it for so long that he gets freakish when he's off them."

But that doesn't even seem that bad. If he was a complete addict, wouldn't he be on harder drugs like coke or meth? How bad can sleeping pills be? "Maybe it wasn't such a good idea to get rid of them."

"I'm all out of ideas," she says. "I've known Andrew basically our whole lives. I'm twenty-eight, so . . . we met when I was fourteen and he was seven. Our parents are old friends, but it wasn't until around then that Andrew and his 'rents moved here from New York City. I know that isn't my entire life but, really, my life only started during my teenage years." She pauses, tucking her hair behind her ear. "I've never seen him not depressed. Except around you, I guess . . . He seems okay with you."

If this were a TV show this would be my cue to hug her. Instead, I shrug and get ready for work, a weird feeling in the pit of my stomach.

Chapter 12

At six o'clock I throw on a lacy white dress and red high heels, deciding that seeing Andrew's performance of *Romeo and Juliet* is a big deal and therefore requires something fancier than my usual black uniform. The University of Toronto is only a short subway ride away from the loft, the campus spread out over beautiful old buildings. I find the Hart House theatre easily and find my seat. I've never seen Andrew act before, only heard him running lines, and it seems important that I should know this part of him as well.

Hours later, when the lights come back on, the room is filled with applause. I stand in the hallway, waiting, and Andrew rushes over and kisses me passionately. "What did you think!" he shouts excitedly, less of a question than a command. He's wearing his usual black pants and t-shirt, the play's period costumes already left behind.

"You were amazing!" I say, reaching for his hand.

He smiles. "Cool. Thanks. So, on to the after party?" When I nod, he says, "Awesome. It's in a nearby residence." He puts his arm around me and we walk through the crowd.

"I hope there's coffee," I say.

Andrew laughs. "It's been, what, one hour since your last caffeine fix?"

"Ha ha. Since this morning, actually."

"Wow, that's a lifetime for you." He opens the door of the building, holding it open so I can walk through, and I follow him into a large room — and when I say large, I mean gigantic. Balloons and streamers of all different colours are taped to the walls, and on first glance I spot the long tables of junk food, pizza and a cake included.

Andrew notices me staring at the food and smiles. "Don't worry. There's plenty of booze. Travis always manages to bring a ton to these parties."

"That's better than coffee, then."

"Always." He leans down to kiss me. "I'm glad you're here."

"Of course. I wanted to see you perform."

"Yeah, well, who can blame you? I am pretty fabulous." He grins and then waves at a red-haired girl. "The Kelster!" he shouts. "You were awesome tonight."

She walks over and I recognize her as his Juliet. "You are ridiculous. I keep telling you how much I want to punch you when you call me that, Andrew."

He rolls his eyes. "Hey, no violence. It's uncool. Come say hi to Brad with me, okay?"

"Who's Brad?" I ask, as more people fill the room. Someone put on loud music — The Killers, it sounds like — and couples are dancing.

They don't answer, the girl grabbing Andrew's arm and whisking him away, heading for a middle-aged male across the room.

When Andrew comes back, he has another girl on his arm. She has blond hair streaked with magenta and is wearing the tightest jeans I've ever seen. "Hey, who are you?" she asks.

I'm completely taken aback. It seems strange, unbelievable even, that someone could be such a huge part of my life, and people who are obviously a huge part of his life too wouldn't know me. But I can't think about this, because the girl is looking at me funny, and I have to answer.

"I'm Raine," I say with more confidence than I feel.

"Have you seen how much he sucks at memorizing?" she asks, twirling her hair around her finger, her nails alternately painted white and black. "Haven't you noticed how defensive this boy gets? He is absolutely freaking adorable, but insult him even jokingly and you'll never hear the end of it."

"He is pretty adorable," I say.

Andrew waves as a group of three guys head

over toward us. They are all dressed the same, in black and red, as if being an actor means following a dress code. I walk over to the food table and fill a paper cup with beer from the keg, drinking it slowly as I watch them from across the room. Maybe it's okay they don't know about me. Maybe Andrew hasn't gotten around to telling them he's met someone.

***

Andrew drapes his arm across my shoulder as we take the subway back to his place after the party. He's pretty wasted, and I feel a buzz from the two beers I had, and from barely eating all day. I try to work up the nerve to ask him why his friends didn't know about me, but every time I try to open my mouth I get too scared.

"Home sweet home," Andrew says, laughing a high-pitched laugh, when we get off at his stop. We walk the two blocks to his loft and he holds my hand the whole time. That is important, I tell myself. This is what counts, the two of us together.

***

I follow him into the loft, up the stairs and onto his bed.

We choose lives the way we choose partners. I have chosen this skinny boy with poetry radiating from his every pore. Who cares if he's the one or not? Who is "the one," anyway? I'm seventeen years old. Maybe I don't care if I find true love anymore. Maybe I'm just figuring out how to swallow one bite of food.

When Andrew leans down and kisses me, I put my whole heart and soul into it. We get wasted and smoke cigarettes and cry over sad songs, and maybe it's all too dramatic, but he *is* an actor. I'm just playing a part. It's the way I have always lived my life, so really, what's the difference? This is just another act, my second — Raine On Her Own Now, scene one, take two. There are no recurring characters except the two of us, the sullen artist cold with romance and the girl he just had to sweep off her feet.

Chapter 13

February becomes mid-February, the coldest winter I can remember. I sit at the kitchen counter staring into a glass of water. Something feels off. It's more than the entire bag of salt and vinegar potato chips I just ate. It's like this poem I read in English last year: this woman thinks she has lost something so she searches her pockets, her purse, her house, but she suffers from such extreme loneliness that even if she touches an object she can't feel it. Even when I'm with Andrew, I still feel so lonely. I wonder if I'll ever feel safe enough when sleeping with someone to stop worrying about my body. I know I did with Dylan, once upon a time in a faraway land of acoustic guitars and English homework. I try to shake the thought of him, because I miss him, and I shouldn't.

"Did you eat all these?"

The question makes me jump. I didn't realize

anyone else was here. I turn to find Sascha staring at me with concerned eyes, holding up the bag of chips. I blush raspberries, a bloodstain on a white sheet. I can't answer. I'm so stupid. It was bad enough to eat those chips, and now I have to be embarrassed about it.

"It's good," Sascha says. I focus on her outfit — army pants and a white blouse, perfectly dishevelled. I wish I could look that good with so little effort. "You should eat."

Yeah, whatever. I go into the bathroom. It's a simple choice. I make sure to run the shower. As I gag and cough I hear pounding on the door. "Raine?" Sascha calls, and suddenly the door swings open and she catches me, on my knees, finger down my throat.

"Okay," Sascha says, slow and calm. "It's okay. Why don't you come upstairs and I'll run you a bath?"

Too embarrassed to speak, I nod. This isn't me, I want to tell her, I don't usually do this. It's too gross. As I follow Sascha up the creaky spiral staircase, I promise myself I will never make myself throw up again.

I won't need to. If you don't eat, you don't need to get rid of it.

Sascha turns away so I can undress, and waits until I'm up to my neck in water in their old-fashioned claw-footed tub to look over. "I'm just going to go ahead and ask: is it so bad you don't get your period anymore?" I nod. I haven't gotten my period in months. "Do you want to talk?" she asks. I shake my head. "Do you want me to leave?"

"I don't mind if you stay."

So we sit in silence, the only sound the slow movement of water in the tub, and I wish I could tell Sascha that she's helping, that I feel better. But I don't.

***

I'm curled up in bed in a sweatshirt and plaid pyjama bottoms when Andrew comes home from class. "Hey," he says, standing in the doorway. "That sweatshirt is pretty massive on you, huh."

I shrug. I'm freezing and it's the warmest thing I have. That bath seems to have made me even colder.

"Sascha said you weren't feeling well today?" he asks. I shrug again. "Is it because of how skinny you are? I mean, you're sick, right?"

"I guess so," I say, deciding to be honest. If anyone would get it, it's Andrew.

"It's really hard for you, right?" he asks. "I mean, living. I don't know. Food is a pretty basic thing. And yet it complicates your world in ways I can't even begin to comprehend."

"Your dad dies when you haven't even finished high school and then your entire life gets screwed up. I think that's the truth."

"No." Andrew shakes his head, coming over

to the bed and sitting down next to me. "*You're* the truth. You are a walking example of the fact that even good-looking girls suffer. I mean, in my opinion, the female species is the most mysterious, awesome thing there is, and if you're just as messed up as I am, well . . . That just rings true to me." He pauses and then asks, "What's it like?"

I know what he's talking about. "You really want to know?"

"Yeah," he says, touching my hand.

"Um," I say, "it's . . . hell, most of the time. Sometimes it makes me feel pretty. Sometimes it makes me feel ugly." And I still can't stop, I think. It's taken hostage of my brain and now I can never get out. "It's kind of hard to describe."

"Can you try?"

I think for a moment. "It's like a high . . . from the stomach pains and headaches and the mania that it produces. And it sounds quiet, but it's an insanely loud quiet, piercing each day with this intensity. It gets so you think you're going to pass out."

Andrew is studying my face, and I wonder what he sees. Do my features look different now that I am describing all of this to him? "Have you ever fainted?"

Be honest, I think. *He wants to know.*

"That's kind of why I'm here," I tell him. "There was this school dance. I passed out. It's scary . . . like the box you have put your life into is suddenly breaking, unable to hold the contents in."

114

"You seem pretty brave, going through that, telling me. There's such strange beauty in pain, you know? Most of the world's greatest art wouldn't have been created if not for all the suffering."

"It's such a cliché, too," I say, feeling a rant coming on, like a train racing up to the subway platform. "I guess that's part of the appeal, to finally belong to some part of the universe. However cliché it might be."

"Well," Andrew says, kissing me so softly, "I think this is where you belong. With me."

I breathe him in, his familiar smell of alcohol, and decide he is right.

We lie down. I hope for sleep, the deepest sleep, right here in the middle of the afternoon. The kind of slumber that erases all of the bad and leaves you with the dreams you have always wished would come true.

***

Sascha is making tea when I come into the kitchen the next morning. I take in her outfit: jean overalls, a red t-shirt, grey Cons. She somehow makes overalls seem cool, something I never thought was possible post-nineties. "Hey," she says. "Want to see my darkroom?"

"There's a darkroom in here?" I ask.

"My bedroom has a walk-in closet, so I converted it into one. I have some stuff I think you would like to see."

I follow her upstairs. The darkroom has a string of photographs hanging up, and when I get a closer look I find that the girl in the pictures is me. When did she take all of these? They seem to cover the entire time I've been living here.

What strikes me at first is how I don't recognize myself. One of the photos is of me sitting on the couch, drinking a cup of coffee. You can see my collarbone. You can see the bones in my knees. I don't see myself like that. I frown at the one next to it, too. I'm staring into space, and my eyes look hollow.

Sascha catches my gaze and smiles weakly. "You know, you're really photogenic. You look pretty fragile, but in an edgy way. I thought I should document it, so you can see for yourself. I didn't think a mirror would do that."

What is this, an artistic intervention? Well, screw her. She can say what she wants. I like what I see in the photographs. There are still areas that need improvement, but for the first time, I look skinny.

"Sascha, it's really none of your business," I say.

She doesn't even flinch. "Chill out, okay? I'm just trying to help."

People say that. But I wonder if it's the truth, or if they just want to rid themselves of their guilt.

***

Friday night Sascha throws a party. A slew of artists come, and they stand in a clump near the window like a flock of black crows, passing around a bottle of red wine. I think this would make a nice photograph, and Sascha must agree, because she pulls out her camera to document it.

"Isn't it amazing?" she asks, eyes glowing. "You can have moments, sure . . . but to be able to freeze them, to go back and relive them again . . .that's the best thing ever."

"Yeah," I say. "I guess it is." I look around for Andrew and spot him sitting on top of the kitchen counter, sharing a joint with Travis. Sascha smiles and walks over to her group. I feel like this amazing night is happening to everyone else and I'm alone. I move over to the staircase and sit down.

A blue-haired boy approaches me, dressed in extremely ripped jeans and a tight white t-shirt. "It's Raine, right?" he asks in a gravelly voice, and I notice his lip ring.

"Yeah. And you are . . . ?"

"Oh. Sorry. I'm Gregory." He puts out his hand. The cute smile that comes along with it makes the gesture less cheesy. I stand up to shake his hand and he says, "Andrew's told me about you. It's nice to meet you."

"Thanks for coming over here. I was feeling like a wallflower." The beer in my hands is making me more confident. "You know who you remind me of?"

"Don't say Tom Delonge," he says, and when

117

I shrug, he sighs. "Every single girl I meet makes that comparison. I know, I know, it's because of the lip ring. But I hate Blink-182."

"How come?" I lean against the wall, expecting a deep response.

"It's just . . . I can't do the manufactured stuff. Anything that gets played on television, I boycott immediately. Even Nirvana was on MTV sometimes, and that really freaks the hell out of me, because then who can you trust? I love Nirvana. God, they speak the language of our whole generation. So Blink-182 . . . I don't know. Maybe it's the numbers-in-the-band-name thing. Maybe it's the pop-punk angle."

"I love Nirvana too," I say.

"A girl after my own heart." Gregory winks, then says, "I'm grabbing a beer. You want another one?" I shake my head, and when he comes back he stands even closer. "Guess who my favourite singer is?" he asks.

"Britney Spears?"

He pretends to gag. "No. Come on. I'm obsessed with Alanis Morissette. Oh, and Joni Mitchell. Those may not seem like guilty pleasures to you, but try explaining your love of philosophical chick music to all the theatre guys."

I laugh. "I'm glad I'm a girl, then, because I can like those singers easily."

"You should be glad you're a girl. You're a pretty cute one." He pokes me playfully in the side, and this hurts a little. "Hey, give me your

118

phone." I pull it out of my pocket and he punches a few numbers into it and hands it back. "There. Now you have my number. Don't be afraid to use it."

"Dude, what do you think you're doing?" Andrew has approached the two of us, and his dark eyes are black again with rage. "You can't just flirt with her."

Gregory laughs uneasily. "What? I am not."

"Touching her, calling her hot —"

"Chill out, man, I didn't call her hot."

Andrew rolls his eyes. "You're one step away from inviting her upstairs to give you a blowjob." His eyes meet mine and he says, "I can't believe you."

"What, I'm not allowed to talk to other guys?" I ask, trying to keep my voice light. I've never been more confused.

"Maybe you're not," he says.

"It's alright, I'll work this out," I tell Gregory. "Go enjoy the party."

"It's not alright. This is ridiculous. I don't need accusations when a friend invites me over." With a harsh look in Andrew's direction, Gregory gingerly takes the beer bottle from my hand and walks toward the bathroom.

"You upset him," I say softly.

"Do I fucking care? I'm the one with you, not him." Andrew wraps an arm tightly around me, and when I pull away he laughs, meanness tracing the edges of it. "You don't want me touching you?

You don't complain when we have sex every night."

"What does sex have to do with anything?" But it isn't what I want to ask — what I want to know is, where did the nice part of him go, and is it coming back anytime soon?

"Everything." Andrew puts his hand over mine, and I hate how much I want him to do this, how even just the smallest touch from him sends electric shock waves through my entire body. "It has everything to do with this. With us."

I go through the rest of the night on autopilot, wondering what the hell is going on. This morning when I stepped onto the scale, I weighed 90 pounds. I feel like I've lost more than just weight. I've lost a dimension, had another layer torn off. Now I'm clearly just a paper doll girl, a mouth moving with hardly any sound at all.

Chapter 14

March. I sit at the kitchen counter, staring into my bowl of Fruit Loops, each colour bleeding into the milk. Sascha comes down the staircase, carrying a huge black tote bag. "Hey," she says, shifting the bag to her other shoulder. "What's up?"

I shrug, stirring the milk with my spoon. "Nothing really."

"Shouldn't you be at work?" She motions to the clock on the microwave. "It's almost twelve."

"I called in sick."

"Hey, why won't you look at me?" she asks, voice wavering.

I meet her gaze. "I just don't feel well. It's not anything big." Sascha opens her mouth and I say, "Please, just don't worry about it, okay?"

"Okay. I'm gonna be late. See you later." When she's gone, I'm thankful.

Andrew walks into the kitchen, yawning, when

I'm pouring my bowl of cereal down the drain. "You seriously need to get how skinny you are," he says. "I mean, an eating disorder is kind of pathetic. It seems like such a high school thing. All these girls squealing about how fat they are, when in reality they're ugly because they're such sticks."

"You think I'm ugly?" I ask.

"Of course that's how you would twist my words around." Andrew puts his hand on his fore- head, like I'm being exhausting. "I don't think that's what you are, I think you're immature when you get like this."

"When I 'get like this'?" I repeat, angry now. "What the hell does that mean? It doesn't just come and go. It's not some decision to like myself one day and hate my body the next. I don't under- stand you."

He comes closer, and I wish he wasn't wearing only a pair of boxers, green plaid ones, because that makes it even harder to fight with him. I wish he wasn't so good-looking. "Maybe I don't under- stand you. Have you thought about that?"

But I haven't.

"Look, you should know. I'm auditioning for a part in a Stratford play. If I get it, I'm going to be moving there in a few months." Andrew sounds so empty of emotion, so straightforward about the whole matter.

I try to phrase this in the most non-pathetic way possible. "What about the loft?" What about me, what about Sascha, what about this thing called a relationship that we have developed?

He just shrugs.

"Where do I fit into this plan?" I ask.

Andrew half-smiles, if you can call it that. "Raine."

"What?"

He reaches for the pot of coffee, his back to me, his shoulder bones prominent. "I have rehearsal," he says.

Right, because he's such a serious actor. Please.

I try to stop myself, but I don't really try that hard, because the air in the room is coming at me all at once and I feel sick. So I end up sitting on the bathroom floor, the door locked, razor in my hand. It's just like it used to be. Cutting is simple. It is what it seems: painful. There is no covering that up, no heavy makeup, no chance for you to get lost. Bandage up the wound, put on a pretty face, and try not to think about how you might have really screwed up this time.

***

I eat one bowl of Cheerios and a few carrots every day for the next week. And then it happens. It happens so quickly I barely have time to catch my breath. But this has been inside of me for so long, its lyrics embedded in my mind, that it's not hard. Maybe that's the worst part, how easy it seems to just give up everything, to push it all away again.

Before I was eating at least a little, and now I take in nothing at all.

***

I fall asleep. When I wake up it's almost nine in the evening. I pull a black dress over my white tank top and wrap myself up in my big grey sweater. I hear noise from downstairs, muffled, like a radio full of static. I walk down the spiral staircase carefully.

At first I can only see Andrew, but it doesn't take long for the scene before me to come into focus — two figures entwined under a blanket.

The girl moves her head slightly to the side, Andrew kissing her neck, and then she notices me. It's Kelsey. His Juliet. "Shit," she says, gently pushing him off of her. "I thought we were alone."

"I thought she was asleep." Andrew sighs.

"Oh, and that would make it okay?" I ask, more angry than hurt.

They both stand up. "Are you guys still . . . ?" she says, raising her eyebrows.

"I thought we were," I say, forcing my voice to stay even.

Andrew shrugs. Maybe he never meant any of it — the words tossed in my direction, the hands he pressed against my heart. "We were never set in stone. Grow up."

"I didn't realize that expecting a guy to stay in a relationship with you was childish," I snap.

He heads for the fridge, grabbing a beer and swigging half of it. "I did you a favour. I let you stay here. You're not my keeper."

Kelsey gives me a helpless look, quickly gathers up her stuff and leaves. Andrew looks at me with empty eyes. "I have this thing to go to. I don't know when I'll be back."

I push open the screen door, heading for the loft's outdoor space. It's just a lawn chair and a low brick wall. The dark makes me feel invisible, just a speck in the world, a tiny star in the sky. I sit on the wall tracing the cuts on my arm, the old ones and the new ones, trying to figure out how I got here.

I move my foot and hit what feels like glass. Kneeling down on the ground I find a pile of empty beer bottles, a few of them with dark pink lipstick prints. I don't wear that shade, and neither does Sascha. How many girls has Andrew brought out here? Has he been cheating on me this entire time? Or is it just a recent development, a sign that he wants to move on, to get rid of me? Time for me to take my cue, bow, and step off the stage.

***

Andrew doesn't come back to the loft until noon the next day. He opens the door and crashes into the room. He looks, in a word, horrible. His black hair is in clumps, his blue t-shirt soaked with sweat. He keeps rubbing his nose. He notices me writing at the kitchen counter but doesn't say hi. He rifles through newspapers on the floor, his eyes stormy, bruised with fatigue. It suddenly registers what he wants so desperately.

"Maybe that's not the best idea . . ." I cringe, aware how lame that sounded, but at a loss for what to do. I follow him as he pushes books away from the shelf and onto the floor.

"Sascha fucking hid them again," he says. "Don't tell me what's a bad idea. Unless you want me to get even more screwed up, you're going to move out of the way and let me go."

I don't move. I can't. This isn't the guy I know, this is someone else entirely, someone meaner than the one whose bed I've been sharing for the past few months.

"What the hell?" Andrew asks, his eyes turning black, worrying me. He is sweating so much, and scratching his right leg, and he keeps holding his stomach as if he is in a ton of pain. "If you have my pills, and this is your idea of a joke . . ."

"I'm not joking," I say weakly. "I just . . ." I reach out to touch his arm, but he throws my hand off harshly.

"I'm going upstairs," he says slowly, "and when I come back down, I'm leaving this apartment." In five minutes, he rushes down the staircase and shakes my arm. "Have you been into my stuff? I had something important in one of my drawers, and now it's gone."

"Of course not!" I say.

He doesn't so much sit on the floor as crumple into a ball. He pulls his knees up to his chest, rocking back and forth, shaking. Then he leans forward and throws up violently. I realize what this is. But withdrawal is something that happens in the movies, not in real life. I can't deal with this. Sascha is showing her photographs at an art gallery tonight. I was planning on going later, but now that plan is shot. So I pick up my cell and dial 911, and when someone answers pull myself together enough to say, "I need an ambulance."

Chapter 15

Hours later, Sascha and I sit in the peach hospital waiting room, talking over stale coffee. It's awful, but I drink it, hoping it will settle my stomach, which is hurting worse than ever.

"The thing about Andrew," she says, "is that he knows what a mess he is and pretty much lives for it. I wonder if he does it on purpose, and then I realize he can't help it. It's, like, programmed into him. He has to push himself, to see how far he can go."

"I thought maybe sleeping pills weren't that bad," I say.

"I thought so too. He used to do harder drugs — coke, ecstasy. Pills were a much gentler contrast."

I nod, taking the last sip of my coffee, which is now not only gross but also lukewarm. "Shouldn't someone be telling us what's going on? We've been here for a while."

"I'll go ask the front desk," Sascha says, standing up slowly and stretching out her arms.

While I wait, I run my hands through my hair, hoping it looks alright. Then I frown. Does it matter what I look like right now?

Sascha comes back after a few minutes. "He's sleeping. The doctor said he has to stay overnight so they can watch him. The doctor also said Andrew needs to seriously think about rehab or an outpatient group. I don't think he's going to give this up without a fight. They mentioned an intervention, but . . ." She sighs and falls into a chair, shaking her head.

I put my hand on her arm. "If you want to go back to the loft, I can stay here. You look pretty worn out."

"Are you sure? I don't mind staying."

"Yeah, I'll be fine. I'll call if something changes."

"Thanks," she says with a tiny smile, then leans over and hugs me. "You're the best. I know why Andrew likes you so much."

Really? I think. *Because I don't. And maybe he's stopped knowing too.*

When she's gone, I decide to visit Andrew. My throat is dry, almost like it's burning. He seems paler than usual, and the fact that he's still alive doesn't comfort me in the least. I'm losing him, however slowly it may be occurring.

I leave the room, sliding down against the wall until I'm sitting and leaning my head on my arms.

What am I really losing? When Andrew pulled me out of my old life and into this new one, I thought it would be different, that he would save me. But nothing's different. So maybe it's me.

***

I spend the night sitting in a chair beside Andrew's bed. When he wakes up, I attempt a smile. "How did you sleep?" I ask, taking in his hospital gown, the dark circles under his eyes.

He sighs, then looks at me. "You can cut the sunshine act." Despite his harsh tone, I can't help but think how gentle he seems as well. The hospital seems to have calmed him down, like the life has been sucked right out of him.

I nod, realizing I have to be the one to repeat the doctor's orders, knowing very well he won't go for it. "This is getting pretty serious now," I say. "I think maybe you should try to stop. The pills, I mean."

Andrew smirks. "Are you fucking stupid? You think this is about pills?"

For a second I'm not quite sure what he means, but then I remember how he asked if I'd taken something from his room, all his anxiety. Sascha said he used to do harder drugs. Maybe he still does.

"They mentioned rehab," I say weakly.

"And aren't we being just the slightest bit hypocritical this morning?" Andrew rolls his eyes.

"I don't say anything if you skip a meal. So what's your deal?"

"You're messing yourself up. It freaks me out. I care about you."

He doesn't answer, just closes his eyes. So I leave. What else can I do?

***

It starts to snow by the time Andrew arrives at the loft. I stand at the window, seeing him climb out of a cab. He walks much slower now, as if he's unsure of where he's going. I watch the flakes, tiny white dreams dancing to the ground. When he pushes the door open, I'm not sure what to expect.

But he just heads upstairs. Sighing, I make myself a pot of coffee and then drink two cups in a row, hoping it'll make me feel more alive. It doesn't. I'm suddenly struck by how lonely this feels, unsure of how Andrew's going to act toward me, unsure of what I'm supposed to do. I have work in an hour, but I decide to skip it, and weigh myself.

85 pounds.

I go upstairs. Andrew is lying on his bed with his hand over his eyes. When I knock softly, he half sits up and glances over at me.

"Hi," I say, and decide to be brave and just ask. "Why did you do that?"

I mean it all, of course: Kelsey, the drugs, the bad moods. He nods and says, "I can barely get my own shit together. I can't worry about yours."

I'm crying, and I feel all jagged edges, no soft-ness in sight.

"Don't cry." This comes out harshly, which makes it happen faster. My head is pounding, my heart is pounding, everything seems to be spin-ning in a million circles. "What the hell is going on with you?" he asks, screaming now, and I press my hand to my forehead. It is way too much noise, a thunderstorm in this tiny room.

"I think I'm sick," I whisper, sliding down onto the floor. "Why didn't it work between us?" My voice cracks mid-question.

"You're not the girl I met in Starbucks," he says. "I might not even be the guy you met. You know what I mean?"

"I expected to fall in love with you."

"You don't love me," he says. "You're still in love with your high school boyfriend."

Dylan. I suddenly miss Dylan so much. Is Andrew right? And I feel it in my bones that he is.

I stand up. "If you don't want me to live here anymore, I'll go."

"Maybe that's a good idea."

This is it. It's all gone now. "Oh," I say.

Andrew laughs meanly. "Why don't you call up Gregory? I'm sure he'd be thrilled to hear from you."

"Maybe I will," I reply. "Maybe I'll go do that right now."

I look around for my stuff. Most of the floor is

covered in my clothes and books, my cell phone on the dresser. I grab my suitcase, so heavy compared to how fragile I feel.

I pass Andrew in the kitchen on my way toward the front door. He just looks at me, his eyes glazed over, and says quietly, "Never promised you a rose garden."

***

80 pounds.

***

I sit on the front steps outside the building, flipping through my cell phone's contact list. I fight the urge to lie down on the ground and fall asleep. I remember this from before, the tightening of my chest, that fearful moment where I feel my eyes shut. But I don't recall the tightening of every other body part, my limbs threatening to break away. My head is going to fall off.

I come across Dylan's cell number. Can't call that. How I wish I could, but what the hell would I say? So, no. Can't call Dylan. Or Katrina. Can't call Matt, either.

I remember Andrew's comment, searching for Gregory's number. He talked to me for a while at the party. Will he talk to me now?

The phone rings a few times. Finally Gregory answers, sounding irritated. "Yeah?"

"Hey. It's Raine."

Pause. "Oh . . . that girl from that thing?" I hear noise in the background, a stereo, someone giggling. "Sorry, could you hold on a second?"

"Okay." I wait, impatient, tugging at my sweatshirt.

He comes back onto the line, coughing. "So, what's up?"

I go blank, rubbing my forehead. "Um. See, Andrew and me had this fight, and . . . I was wondering, could I stay at your place tonight?"

Gregory mumbles to someone next to him, then says, "Sorry . . . it's not a good time. I'm kinda busy."

"Oh," I say, my headache worsening. The line goes dead and I begin to panic.

I spot Sascha walking toward me, looking worried. "Hey," she says. "Are you okay? What's going on?"

"I'm leaving," I say.

"No, that's ridiculous, you don't have to go. Andrew should be the one leaving. It's my place, he's an addict, and enough is enough, you know?" She holds out her hand. "Come on. We're going back inside."

I take her hand and she picks up my bag, which is good, because I can barely stand up. "Whoa," Sascha says, putting an arm around me, and I tear up from how much everything just hurts so much. When she unlocks the loft door, I crouch down and half sit, half lie on the floor, because the couch is way too far away.

Sascha goes upstairs. There is shouting, Andrew's voice the loudest. He swears at her and comes stomping down the stairs, ignoring me and slamming the door behind him as he leaves. She kneels down next to me and says, "Come on. We're going somewhere."

"I just want to sleep," I say.

"Yes, I know, that's why we're going somewhere," she says. "I'm calling a cab. Can you walk?"

I try to stand. I find that I can't catch my balance.

"Okay," she says. "Listen. I'm making an executive decision here. How do you feel?"

I lean against the door and wince. My entire body is killing me. "I feel awful," I tell her.

Sascha kneels down next to me. "The way I see it, you have two options. You can stay like this, feeling terrible, exhausted, and barely able to stand, let alone walk. Or you can come with me and talk to someone. Just talk. If you don't like what they have to say, you can leave. It's a free country, right? But I think you should take a step toward feeling okay again."

I look at her, this girl who has become the closest thing I have to a friend in this new world, if not my only friend these days. She smiles at me sadly. Suddenly, I don't want to be here anymore, in this loft where the boy I thought I loved doesn't want me, in this place where my throat is always sore and my stomach is always too big and there are scars and bruises all over my pale skin.

I thought not eating anything at all would be the solution. But it's not working. I can't stay here and I can't go home, so I give up. If Sascha thinks she can help me, then I'm going to let her.

"Okay," I tell Sascha.

She helps me outside and into a cab. We drive for I don't know how long. When we stop, a beige concrete slab of a building greets us.

It's a hospital.

Epilogue

May. I sit on a bench outside the clinic I've been staying at for the past month and a half. Even the trees are full of promise, white and pink cherry blossoms littering the ground like dreams leftover from winter. Sometimes I feel like I went underground and came back up, and the fog got cleared away. Instead of the scale, my life is monitored by my food intake, and in that way not much has changed. And in that way everything has.

"Hey." I look up to find Dylan walking toward me for our visit. When he called the other day and said my mom told him where I was and that he was wondering if he could see me, I wasn't surprised. It was like I'd been waiting for him. "How are you?"

"I haven't seen you in months, and that's my only greeting?" I ask, trying to be funny. I stand up and hug him. He holds me tight.

"You look good," he says.

"Thanks." I'm able to take the compliment this time. I'm nearing my goal weight, or should I say the clinic's goal weight, of 110 pounds. "You don't look so bad yourself."

"You know, you seem kind of different, but still the same."

I nod, understanding what he means. "You too." His hair a slightly darker brown, his demeanour still so gentle, but a bit tougher, too. He looks so much older. I wonder if he thinks the same of me.

"So, you're here. That's pretty amazing."

"It's overwhelming. But the motto here is to take it one day at a time. I've been writing a lot — we have art therapy every day, and they keep having to give me more notebooks."

Dylan smiles his beautiful smile. "I'm proud of you."

Tears spill onto my cheeks. I smile back, a bit embarrassed, a bit not. He reaches over to give me a hug, tentatively at first, then more comfortably. Doesn't ask why I'm crying. I'm sure he knows.

"I didn't want to die," I whisper.

"You just didn't seem to want to live."

"Not that way," I agree. "Not being afraid of my reflection, being afraid of everything." I wipe my face and motion for him to sit down next to me. He does. "I'm really sorry, you know . . . for how things ended. I could have handled that better. I didn't want to think about it, I just wanted to leave."

Dylan nods. "I knew that. I think that's what made it so hard and so easy for you to be gone. For Katrina, she'd lost her best friend, and she didn't get it. But I knew what you were doing to yourself, and I knew it wasn't about any of us. Just you."

"Hey, I think that's the most honest you've ever been with me. We could be making progress." I hit his elbow, trying to lighten the mood, then frown. "How is Katrina, anyway? And Matt?"

"They're good. Katrina and Adam broke up, so she's been pretty bummed about that. But I think we're all just waiting for graduation. A new start and everything. Hey, what about school? Are you going to finish?"

"Yeah, I'm going to take correspondence courses this summer. My mom wants me to take next year off before applying to university and just get better."

"Sounds like a good plan," he says. "You and your mom are talking?"

"She comes in for family therapy twice a week. It's okay. We're working through our issues, I guess you could say."

Dylan shakes his head. "This year has been crazy."

When you're in the midst of it — all the parties and get-togethers, part of such a happy group of friends — you never think about the finality of it all, of how it will soon be gone. I left earlier, but for Dylan and my old friends, they're just beginning the goodbyes. It makes me feel so much older, like I've gained more than just pounds since being here.

Dylan looks at me and something passes between us, something that has always been there. "I've really missed you," he says.

I know what happens now, I know what it's always been like for us. But just because something is inevitable doesn't mean it has to happen right away.

"If we do this," I say, "it's going to be different."

"Yeah. I know."

"And I'm going to get scared sometimes."

"That's expected."

"Seriously, though. I know how easy it would be for me to go back." I look at him, the years playing across my eyes, a movie about a screwed up girl and the boy who always wanted to save her. She slipped, fell from his grasp, and he grew up. But here they are again . . . there must be a reason. "I just think you should be aware of this."

Dylan is focusing on me, more confident than he used to be. "It's hard, I know, Raine. I wish we could go back, that we could just be us without all of this other stuff, but we'll have to deal with it."

That's my biggest wish, of course, to have never started this battle with the mirror. But those times are gone now. We can never get them back. Sometimes I miss the girl I used to be. It was easier, trying not to need anything. But I know better now.

"Yeah, it is hard. It's hard and I have to work every day just to make sure I don't stare at myself too much. I'll have to deal with this the rest of my life. But you know what? It's life, Dylan."

It's love and it's beauty and it's bones telling your story for you. It's bottling up emotions, non-fat lattes, a love affair with a sad actor. It's saying goodbye to your high school self and learning the rotations of the sun, the way your body works, the way to cry.

The mirror will have to wait. There is no ending here, only a second chance to begin.

Acknowledgements

Sam Hiyate and Alisha Sevigny at The Rights Factory, for believing in me; Carrie Gleason and Sharon Jennings, for editorial guidance; my parents, for supporting my writing since the beginning; my grandma (and her Kingston posse) and my aunt Karen, for being my amazing support group; Alexia Hannis, mentor extraordinaire; Don Hannah and the Tarragon Theatre Young Playwright's Unit; The Sisterhood (you know who you are); Vanessa Campbell and Rachel Geertsema; Anna Dumancic; Tish Cohen and Andrew Pyper, for their kind words; and Eva Graham, Charlie Jurczynski, Nicole Pinto, and Rebecca Roberts, for sharing my happiness about this dream coming true.